ALWAYS THE CHAPERONE

Never the Bride
Book 2

Emily E K Murdoch

ARE YOU SIGNED UP FOR DRAGONBLADE'S BLOG?

You'll get the latest news and information on exclusive giveaways, exclusive excerpts, coming releases, sales, free books, cover reveals and more.

Check out our complete list of authors, too!

No spam, no junk. That's a promise!

Sign Up Here

www.dragonbladepublishing.com

Dearest Reader;

Thank you for your support of a small press. At Dragonblade Publishing, we strive to bring you the highest quality Historical Romance from the some of the best authors in the business. Without your support, there is no 'us', so we sincerely hope you adore these stories and find some new favorite authors along the way.

Happy Reading!

CEO, Dragonblade Publishing

Additional Dragonblade books by Author Emily E K Murdoch

Never The Bride Series

Always the Bridesmaid (Book 1)

Always the Chaperone (Book 2)

Always the Courtesan (Book 3)

Always the Best Friend (Book 4)

Always the Wallflower (Book 5)

Always the Bluestocking (Book 6)

*** Please visit Dragonblade's website for a full list of books and authors. Sign up for Dragonblade's blog for sneak peeks, interviews, and more: ***

www.dragonbladepublishing.com

CHAPTER ONE

"AND HE IS forbidden, Matthews, from having a third, do you hear me?" Charlotte smiled at the butler knowingly, shaking away the hair over her eyes. "The earl has never been able to hold his liquor, and my brother's wedding is not the time to test that."

Matthews bowed and walked from the lawn to the terrace, toward a gentleman who required help. He had managed to finish an entire bottle of port single-handedly and now seemed so intoxicated that he looked unsure whether he had attended the wedding with his wife and children.

Charlotte placed two bottles of wine on the silver platter moving past her in the hands of a footman. Well, the weather had held, which was a miracle for March. The wedding had been perfect. Exactly what her brother deserved.

The lawn of Stonehaven Lacey was clipped to precision, all two hundred guests had arrived on time, and more importantly, to Charlotte's mind, on their best behavior. It was done.

Her smile faded. It was likely to be the only wedding Stonehaven celebrated. After all, the odds of her taking a trip down the aisle were less than none.

"What a stupendous wedding, Lady Charlotte!" A woman Charlotte did not recognize beamed. "And you have undertaken all the details yourself, your new sister was telling me."

Charlotte swallowed the temptation to say it was the only wedding she would probably ever organize and nodded.

"You are a wonder. Is she not a wonder, Mrs. Bryant?"

The most notorious gossip of Bath turned and smiled, walking over to the pair of them. Charlotte's heart sank. Anyone but Mrs. Bryant.

"A lovely wedding," she said in clipped tones. "Of course, nothing can quite compare to Maria's wedding, but then it is unfair to strike the comparison. Why, I heard the other day..."

As always, Mrs. Bryant was soon surrounded by a flock of nosy people eager to hear the latest news and scandal. Trapped in the middle, Charlotte's attention wandered, and she saw them.

Richard and Tabitha. They looked so in love, so happy. Charlotte quashed the bitterness threatening to rise each time she thought about them. She had promised herself she would not be emotional and had come through the whole day without tears. She was not going to succumb.

She needed a distraction.

"You must excuse me," she said to the crowd, none of whom were paying her any attention, eyes on Mrs. Bryant. Breaking free from the crush, she crossed the lawn and brought her new sister into her arms.

"I could not be more pleased to be proved wrong," laughed Charlotte. "It is clear to anyone who loves Richard that he is absolutely besotted with you."

Tabitha laughed, her green eyes sparkling in the afternoon sun as Charlotte released her. "I do not think I could have asked for a better husband, nor a better welcome into a family. Thank you for being my bridesmaid, Charlotte. I would not have had the courage to marry today without you."

Charlotte knew Tabitha meant her words kindly, but it hurt to see such a young thing become the new Duchess of Axwick, her mother's title. Tabitha was barely five and twenty. Here she was, ten years older, and no closer to marriage than she had been when Tabitha's age. "Well, it's certainly better than being a chaperone."

Tabitha opened her mouth, but before she could speak, a young woman approached them with a nervous smile.

"Lady Charlotte? I beg a moment of your time and apologize for the intrusion."

Charlotte's false smile did not waver. She knew what this interruption was about. "Yes, Miss Darby?"

Her nervous smile broadened, and she started speaking quickly as though she would lose heart if she did not speak in a rush. "It is only that I thought you may be attending *The Magic Flute* in Bath next week, and I would very much like to go. But my father is too unwell to leave the house, and I have been asked by William Lennox, the Duke of Richmond, to attend. You must have met him and his brother, but of course, I may not go alone. It would not be seemly, so I was wondering if you would accompany me as my chaperone?"

There it was. The inevitable request, and Charlotte had been so sure she would get through the wedding without one! It hurt, for she had acted in that capacity for four or five couples last Season. She did not consider Charlotte a companion but an old woman who would ensure nothing untoward occurred. But did Miss Darby have to make it so obvious?

Miss Darby had not said the word *spinster*, but she may as well have. Charlotte bit down the retort that she should ask Lady Romeril to do it, for she was over sixty and definitely beyond the suggestion of scandal.

In her most genteel voice, she said, "Of course, Miss Darby. I would be delighted to accompany you. Please send round the details in a notecard, so I shall ensure not to engage myself for anything else that evening."

"Oh, Lady Charlotte, you can have no idea how happy you make me!" Miss Darby's eyes were wide and so was her mouth. "And to think before I thought of you, I could not conceive of anyone else who would accompany me, for you know Miss Seton is too young, and Mrs. Coulson is engaged that evening. After I saw you in the church today, I thought..."

Was there any point in trying to stem the flow of those well-meaning but excruciating pleasantries? Charlotte stared as Miss Darby allowed her mouth to run away with her, trying to ignore the hurt on Tabitha's face. Without saying a word, she reached out and squeezed her new sister's hand.

"And how is the Duchess of Axwick feeling?" Her brother, Richard, had crept up behind Tabitha and wrapped his arms around his new bride, murmuring in her ear.

Tabitha flushed with pleasure, and Charlotte turned away. She could not bear the happiness on their faces. At her time of life, the possibility of marriage was over. A life of chaperoning was ahead of her.

"–will tell the gentlemen. Thank you again!"

Charlotte blinked. She had paid so little attention to Miss Darby; she had not noticed her raptures had ended. The lady curtsied and returned to her group.

The group was predominately ladies, all young, pretty, with the most ridiculous bonnets of the latest fashions. Accompanying them were two gentlemen. They were obviously brothers, and one could see it in their faces, the same eyes and the same curve of the mouth. They even held themselves similarly, rather stiffly, as though a wooden board had been shoved up their shirts and breeches.

Charlotte stifled a giggle. One of the brothers was taller than the other, and more handsome, in her opinion. More strength in the jaw, more breadth in the shoulder. More presence than some gentlemen had and others strived for.

What would it be like to be a woman standing with them? Laughing away without a care in the world, certain you are going to find a match and end the Season married?

And what would the gentlemen be thinking? The shorter of the two was speaking, telling a story, and capturing their attention. Her gaze flickered over to the taller. What was he like? Did he enjoy societal pleasantries, or was he as bored as she was?

His gaze suddenly met hers, and Charlotte gasped as a flash of something—heat, intrigue, interest, she could not tell, sparked across her body. He was looking right at her as though he had sought her out in a crowd and finally discovered her. His eyes were blue, and he smiled.

Heat warmed her cheeks, and she immediately dropped her gaze. What must he think of her, staring at a gentleman?

Richard and Tabitha had disappeared, but a few people stood around talking, and she quickly attended to their conversation. Anything to distract her from that look.

"—and so I told them, I do not care whether it is a park or a garden or the street!" A woman was saying in an impressive voice, and two others were nodding. "If you are going to be seen in that gentleman's company again, I beg you to take a chaperone. I mean to say, without a chaperone, who can tell what truly occurred!"

Charlotte's heart sunk. Of course, it was a conversation about chaperones. Fate would permit nothing else. As Admiral Jenkins spoke to give his commendation to the woman's words, Charlotte risked a glance.

He was still staring, and his smile was wider.

He could not be staring at her. There must be a young, beautiful lady behind her. Her jaw relaxed as she turned to look.

There was no one behind her.

This was unprecedented; no gentleman had ever looked at her like that! Charlotte felt uneasy, desperate to walk away but with no control over her feet. She was the one always in the background, not the woman in the front!

"What say you, Lady Charlotte?" The admiral was glaring as

though she was supposed to heartily endorse his words and had missed her cue. "As a seasoned chaperone, you must agree it is vital for our young people to have an older, wiser presence in their courting?"

Charlotte had inherited few things from the Axwick line for which she was thankful, and one of them was her temper. It was her father's temper and no matter how she tried to suppress the flames, it rose hot and spluttering, like a fire with too much fuel.

"Are you asking my opinion as someone no longer young?" she asked curtly, a mirthless smile on her face.

The admiral stomped his feet. "Well, I did not exactly mean…"

Face still hot from the gaze of the tall gentleman, she decided to rescue the admiral and place him once more on solid ground.

"You must excuse me," she said with a deep curtsey, "I have just seen something needing my attention."

The man's relief was palpable, but it was nothing to the confusion whirling in Charlotte's mind as she stepped away and saw the unknown gentleman was still looking at her. His smile threw his features into an even more favorable light.

She had to get away from this strange man. What could he possibly want with her?

She stumbled as she stepped off the lawn and onto the terrace and was immediately accosted.

"Ah, Lady Charlotte! What a wonderful wedding, do you not think?"

It was Miss Theodosia Ashbrooke, the well-known matchmaker, all the way from London. Charlotte tried to smile, anything to hide her confusion.

"Yes, it was," she managed. "I do apologize, Miss Ashbrooke, please excuse—"

"Yes, I think it is my third favorite," Miss Ashbrooke said thoughtfully. "I say so advisedly, for all my clients invite me to their weddings. Why, the other day—"

"You must excuse me," said Charlotte firmly, stepping around the matchmaker and aiming for the dining room.

"Lady Charlotte!" Jacob Beauvale, Lord Westray, grabbed her hand, and if he had not been such an old friend of the family, she would have hit him for so irritatingly stopping her in her tracks once more. "A favor, old thing. I have a sweet miss I wish to have to dinner, but blasted etiquette, I need another female in the house. Are you available?"

"My calendar is booking up quickly, Westray," Charlotte said tartly, wrenching her arm away and trying not to think of those piercing blue eyes. "You will have to…" Her voice died as she saw the disappointed look on his face. "Damn it, Westray, you know how I feel about chaperoning."

His eyes glittered. "How you love it so much, you mean, when it means helping out a friend who has stood by your brother's side."

"You blaggard," sighed Charlotte. Anything to get away. "Give the details to Matthews, and I will see if I am available."

It was infuriating being unable to find a quiet place where she could think in her own home! But Richard had insisted on the guest list, and though Stonehaven Lacey was a large manor, it was unaccustomed to hosting hundreds.

Wherever Charlotte turned, there were people, well-wishers, gossips, footmen, the curious, the nosy, and the downright irritating. All she wanted was a minute to sit quietly and think. To treasure that moment when her eyes had met his.

And then she thought of it. Within moments, she was turning a handle and seeing with relief that the music room was empty.

She shut the door and leaned on it. Peace at last. As soon as Richard and Tabitha left for their honeymoon, she was going straight to Bath. How strange that, today, Bath was the quieter option!

The large pianoforte was in the center of the room, the heavy linen cover faded in patches. The door to the garden was open, but the music room was on the other side of the house from those celebrating her brother's wedding. No one would find her here. Throwing open the doors, Charlotte breathed in the clean spring air and slumped onto the piano stool.

She should have expected it. She should have known a wedding was the perfect opportunity for young people to meet potential suitors, for young ladies who had just come out this Season to hunt for husbands.

At five and thirty, she had seen the same dance over and over again. Some of her peers, ladies of title and fortune who had come out with her, were starting to think of matches for their own children.

Charlotte pushed up the lid of the pianoforte, allowing her hand to rest gently on the keys. There was no use in denying it. She was a spinster, and her only role in the marriage market now was to help others.

Her fingers fell naturally into a Mozart sonata. It had been one of the first pieces Mr. Portland, their tutor, had taught her. A natural smile crept across her face at the memory of his frustration, eventually admitting politely—for a tutor did not scream with irritation at the daughter of a duke—that she would never be much of a musician.

All these years later, it turned out she was not much of a lady of society either.

"I am almost sure I know that tune."

CHAPTER TWO

I T WAS DISGRACEFUL manners to appear bored before a lady. William Lennox knew this even before he had ascended to the title of Duke of Mercia.

But that did not make it easier when Miss Darby warbled on about all of the delightful beaus at Almack's.

"—but then, as a doctor, of course, he is rather busy with his patients," she simpered, throwing a look up to William. "It is difficult to shake off Mr. Prander, however, who…"

Keep your smile steady, William told himself. After all, it wasn't possible for Miss Darby to continue talking indefinitely without drawing breath. Was it?

A quick glance at his brother, John, told him it was. When gentlemen of good fortune and name looked at Miss Darby the way his brother was now—eyes glazed, a winning smile—she would continue until she ran out of breath.

What a day. He had not expected a wedding would be the place to be barraged by young ladies and their mamas, but it was worse than the Pump Room for silly chits looking to secure a rich and preferably titled husband.

When the letter from the Court of St. James had arrived, informing him he had inherited a title, he had been concerned about financial responsibilities. Little had he known that siring an heir would take precedence.

So, to the marriage market he had come, and apparently every woman under thirty, too. William smiled, despite himself. Well, hadn't he earned it?

What a shame all these young ladies were all so insipid.

"No, I do not believe you, Miss Darby!" His brother laughed.

William laughed too late. John, or the Marquess of Gloucester as he was now, glanced at him with a questioning look, but William shrugged it away. How could he explain his discontent?

There were undoubtedly gentlemen who dreamt of waking up one morning with a title, but they would be fools. It had certainly entertained John. But William had never sought that life, and discovering that his own desires, opinions, even direction in life would now have to bow to the heavy burden of his new name was tiresome beyond words.

What he would give for some real conversation.

"Mercia, are you feeling well?" John pulled his arm, taking him outside the circle of ladies as Miss Darby went to speak to the bride. "You are hardly attending to Miss Darby."

"Is it little wonder?" retorted William. "First the boredom of London, then the repetition of Bath, and now this? I had thought flirtation and courting was something to look forward to after the war, but this is just irritating."

His brother did not look convinced. "You jest, surely. Miss Seton was a delight to speak with, and Miss Tilbury, perhaps too much so!"

William grinned at his brother. Five years younger, he may have been through Sandhurst, but he had never seen the battlefield, and it showed. "Gloucester, these chits are inane, there is no intelligence in them at all."

"Who wants intelligence?" John had a spark in his eyes that William knew all too well. "We are surrounded by beauty…"

"—but nothing of substance." William sighed. "I know it was right and proper that we showed our faces here today."

"Your face," John interrupted. "Everyone wants the new Duke of Mercia, not his younger brother."

William paused, looking into his brother's eyes. Was that bitterness, a hint of envy in his voice?

"Ah, Your Grace, I have good news!" Miss Darby was back, and she was beaming. "I have spoken with Lady Charlotte, sister of the Duke of Axwick, and she is perfectly amenable to act as chaperone for our plan!"

William coughed in the awkward silence. "Plan?"

Miss Darby's smile faded. "To the opera. *The Magic Flute*. You invited me."

It all came rushing back to him, the spare tickets and the impetuous invitation he had made not ten minutes before.

"The opera!" he said, trying to inject some merriment into his words. "What a kind offer of Lady Charlotte."

"She is indeed immensely kind," warbled Miss Darby. "I was concerned at first she may not be disengaged, for she is in the top set of society in Bath, but when I asked her…"

Well, at least Miss Darby had this for her, thought William. Whoever married her would never be short of conversation. She was talented enough to continue all by herself, without needing anyone else to contribute.

Another yawn threatened to surface, but he quashed it. He was in polite society, and it wouldn't do to be rude. But then, what did it matter? There were still countless, tedious women whom he had not met yet.

Allowing his gaze to wander lazily across the wedding scene, something stopped it in its tracks.

A woman. She was tall, slim, with chestnut hair and gray eyes, dressed in the grayest gown he had ever seen. She was watching him.

Realizing she had been caught, she looked away with a pretty blush, eyes downcast. William stared. It was the bridesmaid from the wedding, the sister of the groom. Lady Caroline, perhaps—no. Lady Charlotte, that was what Miss Darby had said.

Lady Charlotte. He had barely noticed her before, for she was wearing such drab clothes. Out here in the fading sunlight, everyone else looked overdressed with their diamonds and feathers and furs. She looked perfect.

She was listening to an admiral, by the look of his dress uniform. The more William looked, the more strange it was that he had not been drawn to her. No, she did not capture the eye of every gentleman, but she was elegant. No young thing, but a woman of maturity and strength—and with a figure to match.

Parts of William stirred that had not been awoken by Miss Darby.

Lady Charlotte looked at him again. So, she had noticed him, too. All the better.

There was that blush again, and it was deeper this time. After speaking a few quiet words with her companions, she stepped away from them and started moving toward the house.

Ah, so she wanted to speak with him. She could be just as dreary as the rest of them. Better to find out now if she had any wit about her, then he could dismiss her from his mind.

William stepped forward to follow her, but Lady Charlotte surprised him. She did not slow down or change her direction to allow him to catch up.

She kept walking and had not intended him to follow her at all. She was actually going into the house!

William chuckled and received some strange looks from the ladies around him who were still, remarkably, listening to Miss Darby.

Not every woman was all about the tricks. He shook his head, thrilled by the surprise. What an intriguing woman, beautiful but with no flirtation in her. No assumptions, no rule-breaking. Just a woman.

"Miss Darby," he found himself saying, unsure exactly why he was asking and ignoring the affronted look on her face as he interrupted her. "Tell me about Lady Charlotte."

"Lady Charlotte?" Miss Darby frowned. "Why?"

Too late, William remembered it was not gentlemanly to appear interested in another woman when speaking with a woman you have just engaged for a social outing.

"Because I would like to thank her for accompanying us next week," he said with a hint of a smile as he took her hand. "Otherwise, I could not enjoy the pleasure," he gave a gentle caress across her fingers, "of your company."

Miss Darby's eyes widened. William was almost disappointed in her. So easily won.

"Oh, Lady Charlotte," she said breathlessly. "She is not much to speak of, truth be told. She is ancient, of course, but good about helping out us young things. She has acted as chaperone for two of my friends, and one of them is now married. Poor Lady Charlotte, this is the closest she will ever get to marriage!"

She laughed, and her friends joined in, but William did not. His estimation of Miss Darby, never high, sunk lower.

"You must excuse me," he said with a bow, and without waiting to hear their replies or his brother's question, he started walking toward the house.

If he had not been trying to avoid Miss Theodosia Ashbrooke's eyes like blazes as he approached the terrace, he would not have changed direction. That would not have brought him to the east side of the house, and that probably meant he would not have heard the pianoforte. The music was coming from a door ajar on the side of the house.

William reached the door and saw Lady Charlotte with her back to him, seated on the stool of a pianoforte, picking out what sounded like a truly awful rendition of a Mozart sonata.

She tilted her head, and William caught sight of her graceful neck. He found himself captivated by her mature grace, not a girl who had only left the nursery yesterday.

Well, he was not going to find a better opportunity.

"I am almost sure I know that tune."

His words came out a little hoarse, and she stiffened, turning around to stare. Unlike every other encounter with a gentlewoman since ascending to the title, William found his easy manner and wit suddenly lacking.

"And you are?" Her tone was not unfriendly, exactly. More like ice.

William swallowed. This was not exactly how he had imagined this conversation. "William Lennox, Duke of Mercia."

He bowed. She was evidently not impressed by the title.

Why would she be? Daughter of a duke and sister of a duke, he had been foolish to think his title would make any difference.

She did not even rise from her piano stool, but inclined her head and said quietly, "Lady Charlotte St. Maur."

Part of William hoped she would extend her hand, giving him the opportunity—and the excuse—to enter the room. But she did not.

"You should give a recital later this evening," William said with a winning smile. A curl of hair fell across her cheek, and it made him want to sweep it out of her eyes and pull her into his arms.

Why was he having such a physical reaction to this woman?

"No, thank you," she said stiffly, dropping her gaze. "I do not enjoy being in public."

William smiled. "No, you do not. Neither do I. Are you enjoying the day?"

She looked up, but the slight frown did not disappear. "Yes."

Raising a hand to the handle of the door, William fiddled with it. Anything to break the tension between them, a tension he did not understand. Why did he find it impossible to step into the room—and why did he want to so badly? Why did she look both intrigued and frightened to see him there?

"I am glad of it. Very much so," he managed. "But I have been remiss in not getting to know my hostess better. Do you think I will have the chance later on this evening?"

"I am sure the Duchess of Axwick will speak with you soon."

William blinked. Hell's bells, she was lovely. What he wouldn't do to—no, he must focus. "I meant you."

She scrunched up her nose as though she had smelled something distasteful. "Are…you are not aware of the change in precedence?"

Heat washed through him. "Precedence?"

Lady Charlotte nodded. "You see, before my brother Richard married, I was the most senior female in the Axwick line. Once he married, his bride Tabitha, Duchess of Axwick, takes my place. I am no longer the mistress of this household."

His jaw tightened. It was one thing to have to receive a lesson in precedence because you were not born to a certain place in the world, but it was quite another to lose that place.

"And do you mind?"

Perhaps it was his bold question. Perhaps it was the lack of pleasantries. Or perhaps it was because there was no guile in his words. Whatever the reason, Lady Charlotte looked him in the eyes for the first time since he had seen her by the pianoforte.

"You ask many questions for someone I have just met."

It was that look, so innocent and yet inviting, that spurred him on. Stepping into the room and with his voice low, he said, "Time can solve that problem."

She did not move, but her eyes narrowed. "You are well-rehearsed, Your Grace."

William laughed dryly. "Perhaps, but then I have studied the steps of elegant conversation closely. Do you not think that many in our society would have done well to do the same?"

There was a rather knowing look in her gaze as she replied, "You speak very decidedly for a gentleman so recently raised to a title."

Well, of course, she would know that—all the true nobility had known each other from birth. Were they not all related, somehow?

The news of his ascension must have caused ripples through society far more than he could guess.

William took another step closer to her. "I may not have been born with blue blood, my lady, but it turns out you can inherit it."

Was that a flicker of a smile? Whatever it was, Lady Charlotte controlled herself immediately. "Some would argue true breeding cannot be inherited."

"If land, title, home, and horses can be, why not nobility?" he countered. "I think manners are taught, rather than entrenched in the bone."

His gaze raked across her face. She had not asked him to leave. She was watching him as a rabbit watched a hawk, almost certain she was prey, but wondering whether, if she just stayed still, he would leave her alone.

"I-I do not know," she said, faltering. "I have given little thought to it."

"You have not needed to," William said calmly. There was magnetic energy to her, even without her trying. He felt every inch of himself want to be closer to her, to hear her speak. "You, my lady, have been blue-blooded from birth."

She seemed to distrust him. "And you were a soldier."

He could not hide his surprise. "Ye gods, woman, are you a soothsayer?"

Heat seared his cheeks. He had always spoken his mind, and John had teased him for it—but to speak so in front of a lady!

A lady who was laughing.

"M-my lady, you must accept my apologies," William stammered. "I did not mean to—I am sorry if I have offended."

"Offended?" She sat up straight as her laughter subsided, and the joy in her eyes did not disappear. "Your Grace, you remind me so much of my grandfather, I was shocked into laughter. I am more concerned that I have offended you."

Sweet relief poured through his soul as he took another step. He was standing right before her now. If he wanted, he could reach out and touch her.

"Your grandfather?"

She nodded. "He was an admiral and continuously startled my mother, his daughter, with his loud voice and abrasive thoughts. I rather liked him."

"It is strange how memories like that resurface after many years," he said quietly. "But I am more interested in the memories I am making now."

Did she understand him? Her eyelashes fluttered as her gaze dropped. "*Now*, Your Grace?"

"The sight of a beautiful woman. One whom I have managed to make smile."

She immediately rose. "I look forward to *The Magic Flute* with your Miss Darby, Your Grace. If you do not mind, you must excuse me, I need to find Matthews about—oh!"

William gasped, too. The moment he had taken her hand, something stiffened in him, and not only his manhood, which had been twitching ever since he first caught her staring. No, it was a more deep, primal reaction.

William stroked her hand as he had with Miss Darby, but this was different. Lady Charlotte was different. "I look forward to it, too."

She stared, and her lips parted. She leaned toward him, and William thought for a moment that she was going to allow him to kiss her.

Instead, she leaned near his ear and whispered, "I shall give Miss Darby your regards." Then she left him alone in the music room.

CHAPTER THREE

N O MATTER WHAT she did, Charlotte could not get that strand of
hair to stay put.

She sighed, breath misting the looking glass in the crisp April
morning. It was ridiculous. She had never been concerned with her
looks, even when attending her first Season. She was far more
interested in seeing the people she had heard so much about from her
oldest brother, Arnold.

Her nose scrunched. *Arnold.* Well, they were well rid of him.

And tonight was nothing special. Her mind unwillingly traipsed
back to the week before.

"I look forward to it."

Charlotte started and almost dropped her diamond earbobs, fingers tightening around them.

The Duke of Mercia. She was not going to get herself tangled over
him, no matter how handsome he was. Not that she had noticed.

Blowing out a frustrated breath and concentrating this time, she
carefully put on her mother's diamond earbobs. They had been her
favorite legacy, though she rarely wore them. There was little point.
She was typically the third person at the opera, the third to dine, the
third for a walk. An accessory to a courting couple. Largely ignored
but necessary.

She examined her reflection critically. Well, her gown was at least
five seasons old and starting to be truly out of fashion. Her hair was

completely untamable. But the diamonds were perfect.

It was too much to hope that she and the duke would have a conversation, especially after she had been so dismissive. He had frightened her with his intensity, which drew her to him in a way she did not like.

That was what she kept telling herself.

"The carriage is here, my lady."

Matthews's voice echoed up the stairs, and Charlotte smiled grimly in the looking glass. It was time. Grabbing her pelisse, she walked downstairs to see the butler holding her reticule for her.

"The Axwick diamond earbobs," he nodded. "I highly approve, my lady."

Charlotte blushed. Matthews meant well, had meant well for all twenty-five years he had served her family. He was practically one of them. But that did not explain…

"Matthews," she said briskly, taking the reticule, "may I ask you a question?"

The butler raised an eyebrow.

"Why did you decide to return with me to Bath? I would have thought Richard and Tabitha needed you at Stonehaven Lacey."

If she had not known Matthews so well, she could have missed the flicker of pride across his face.

"They did inquire whether I would remain, my lady," he said delicately, "but I made a promise to your mother that I would keep you under my care until…until you had a household of your own."

Charlotte flushed. Love for her mother, embarrassment that her butler thought five and thirty was not sufficient age to look after oneself, and the hint at matrimony.

A knock on the front door interrupted them. Matthews stepped forward to open the door to reveal a shivering footman. "The carriage is waiting for Lady Charlotte."

She sighed. They had managed quite well without a carriage for over three years while the family finances were in disarray. Having one now felt strange and more often than not, she left it in the country. One was always at the beck and call of the horses, never the other way around. She must send it back to Richard, where the horses could enjoy the countryside.

"I am ready," she said and smiled at the butler again. "Thank you, Matthews."

Miss Darby's lodgings with her father were two streets away, so Charlotte gained little silent respite before she was joined by her night's charge.

"But of course, I had seen Miss Tilbury had worn a similar gown, and so I wondered whether it was quite the thing, but I asked my father, and he said he knew the Earl of Marnmouth well, and so as long as my dressmaker…"

Charlotte could not help but smile. The bright eyes and flushed cheeks of Miss Darby were much easier to absorb in the evening dark of the carriage. She could remember her first time attending an opera, her first balls, the dinners she was permitted to go to by her father. So much excitement, so much promise.

Her smile faded as the carriage jolted around a corner. Those evenings were almost twenty years ago. She had come out to a different type of Season, with different nobility, dances, and novels in fashion. Miss Darby may not even have been born then.

The carriage came to a stop.

"Oh, are we here! Goodness, that was no time at all, and I have barely had the chance to tell you…"

To Charlotte's relief, the carriage door opened, and a hand with a golden ring extended toward her. It had a swirled letter *M* around what appeared, upside down, to be a bird. A magpie? Charlotte took the hand but dropped it immediately. Even through her silk gloves, she could feel the heat pouring from the hand to hers.

"Are you feeling well, Lady Charlotte?" Miss Darby's face was a wash of concern.

Charlotte swallowed. It was her imagination. It was not possible to feel such intensity through gloves! The hand was still outstretched, and she took it again, trying to ignore the rush of warmth that once again filled her. She stepped out—into the waiting smile of William Lennox.

"Good evening, my lady," he said.

Rarely did Charlotte have no response. She dropped his hand immediately but could still feel the spark of his touch. As though they had held hands for an age.

"I trust you are well?" He was still grinning, almost laughing as if he had told a joke.

Charlotte steeled herself. She would not allow herself to be a joke. The street was busy, teeming with opera lovers excitedly awaiting their turn to enter the building and find their seats, and it was time for a new set of lovers to take their place.

"Here, Miss Darby, let me help you." Charlotte turned and offered a hand for her young companion, who tripped on her gown as she exited the coach and was caught in the strong arms of the duke.

"Oh, Your Grace, how embarrassing for me!" Miss Darby fluttered her eyelashes.

Charlotte scrunched her nose and tried not to tut aloud. *Really!* She did not consider herself a prude, but such behavior—and on the street, too, where anyone could see!

She cast a quick glance at the duke to see his response to such a flirtatious move and was surprised to see Miss Darby already out of his arms and standing between the two brothers.

"Shall we?" The duke indicated toward the opera house doors, offering his arm, which Miss Darby gladly took.

As the couple walked, Charlotte fell in behind them alongside the Marquess of Gloucester.

"My, what a wonderful place! And to think, though my father and

I have been in Bath a month, we have not been here! It does not seem quite right that we should come all this way for the Season and not even try some of its delights," Miss Darby began ahead of them.

Charlotte sighed and forced a smile. "Good evening, Lord Gloucester."

"Good evening, Lady Charlotte, and please call me John. I have had the title for but a short time, and it does not sit well with me," he said in a low tone. "It was only last year my brother and I even discovered we had a little blue in our veins, and I am just a simple soldier."

He grinned, and Charlotte nodded. He had the same easy manner as his brother—a consequence, perhaps, of not being raised in the rigor and restrictions of her class.

"Well then, John," she said lightly, "if you are truly happy for me to speak so familiarly, I will call you by your Christian name, though it is rather shocking."

He chuckled. "Fear not, I will continue to speak to you as Lady Charlotte, as decorum insists. If I forget, whack me on the nose. It is the only way I will learn."

Charlotte laughed. She had not expected any merriment this evening, and though he had none of the attraction of his brother, she could not deny John was good company.

His attention was now focused before them. "Have you ever seen anything so lovely as Miss Darby?"

The words could have been taken as an ironic quip, but as they walked into the candlelit entranceway, all covered in red velvet and gold, Charlotte saw, to her surprise, that there was sincerity in his words and the flush of excitement in his cheeks.

She raised an eyebrow.

"You do not need to speak," John said ruefully, "I know what you will say. It is shameful to say such things about the young lady my brother is courting."

His jaw tightened as his eyes flickered over to his brother's companion. Charlotte followed his gaze, and as Miss Darby tilted back her head to laugh at something the duke had said.

Charlotte took the younger man's arm. "If something is on your heart, John, then you should say it. I would not wish you to miss out on a chance of happiness for an excess of decorum."

They ascended the steps as Miss Darby leaned closer to the duke, and Charlotte felt the tension in John's arm.

"If you do not say something, you will regret it," she murmured so only her companion could hear her.

John turned to her as they were ushered toward the box the duke had reserved. "You are right, Lady Charlotte, and I thank you. Perhaps I will have enough courage tonight."

Once again, she was the one giving out advice. Four marriages formed through her chaperoning, but had she ever taken her own advice?

No. Embarrassed to put herself forward when young, unwilling to when the family fortunes had disintegrated, unable to when she sacrificed her dowry to restore the family name...any gentlemen callers who had ever considered her received little encouragement.

She could not regret most of it. The Axwick estate was solvent again, and that was all that mattered for those frightening months when sale—*sale!*—of the Stonehaven Lacey estate seemed not possible, but a probable solution to their problems.

But that had all changed when Richard had married, and she was once again a chaperone.

"Good evening, my lady."

Charlotte started as an usher bowed low, welcoming her to the box. She had not been attending to her steps nor surroundings.

"Thank you," she said graciously, inclining her head. There were four seats placed in the box, luxurious and comfortable, quite unlike the shilling seats below, already filling up with a noisome chatter.

She knew the decorum: she would sit on the left with Miss Darby beside her, the duke—she must remember to call him Your Grace—would sit beside her, and John at the other end.

Her gown swished as she moved around to place herself on the left, and before Miss Darby could move, the duke placed himself beside Charlotte.

"Come, Miss Darby, sit by me," he said jovially as Charlotte attempted to find the words to explain that this was not appropriate. "And John on the end."

Charlotte frowned. She had to say something; this was highly irregular. The entire point of her presence was to be beside Miss Darby, a check to the courting couple.

Anything could happen, untoward and unbecoming, and she would be totally unaware.

"Miss Darby, I think," she began, but then caught sight of John's face. He was happy and glanced at Miss Darby with a reverential look.

Well, she could not have predicted this, but in a way, it made sense. Here was Miss Darby with the duke on one side and the marquess on the other. A place much admired and sought after by the ladies of the *ton*.

This was Miss Darby's chance to talk with both brothers and see which took her fancy. And John's chance to make himself known to her, to charm her.

Charlotte fought the bitterness rising in her throat. It was unbecoming to be envious of a young woman like Miss Darby. She had committed the crime only of having two men want her.

Charlotte looked out at the empty stage with unseeing eyes. To think such a thing really happened. She would have to swallow her irritation and ensure Miss Darby did not expose herself to any gossip from the ever-present eyes of society.

The curtain rose, and she applauded as the conductor, a man with the most impressive mustache she had ever seen, bowed. The stage was suddenly filled with people, and the opera began.

Charlotte was transfixed. Music always had a special place in her heart, even though she had little talent herself. The melody rose in a crescendo, and her pulse rose with it, utterly captivated by the harmonies. The heat in the building and the copious candles illuminating the stage made the place overwhelming. She absentmindedly removed her gloves, placing them in her lap.

Whispers distracted her from the stage. John and Miss Darby were talking away to each other, their hands impossibly close without touching.

Charlotte smiled. *Bad luck, Your Grace, but I think your brother has won this one.*

The thought of the duke reminded her he was seated beside her, and a prickle of discomfort moved over her skin. She had been so lost in the music that she had forgotten him. But now she was conscious of his presence, and she could not block it out. He was lounging back in his seat, as though he had never been anywhere more comfortable.

As she tried not to look around, he leaned toward her. "And what are you smiling about, Lady Charlotte?"

She shivered. "Nothing."

She hoped the sparse reply, along with its icy tone, would dissuade him from continuing the conversation, but it did not.

"My word," he said with a raised eyebrow Charlotte pretended she could not see, "you must be easily entertained if *nothing* can make you smile. Why come to the opera at all?"

She glanced at him, a frown beginning to form. It appeared that, despite the entertainment, he wanted to converse with her.

Miss Darby giggled, the sound muffled inadequately by her hands.

Charlotte spoke in her most prim voice, "Why not ask Miss Darby what has made her laugh, Your Grace?"

He leaned closer to her, and Charlotte moved back. It was not right, being this close to a gentleman in public.

"I wish you would call me William," he whispered. "You call my brother, John."

If she had been hot before, it was nothing to the new rush of embarrassment. Charlotte turned with her mouth open, ready to defend herself, but all the eloquence of her breeding escaped her.

"I did not—it was not my suggestion. Your brother asked…"

Her splutters were louder than she had intended, and the duke laughed. "We both ascended to these ridiculous titles at the same time, and neither of us are comfortable with them. Come on, William is hardly a difficult name to pronounce or remember."

She hesitated. It was all very well for a marquess to request the use of his Christian name, and John was so…well, so unassuming.

Not like his elder brother. William was imposing, taller, a stronger presence, something animalistic in the way he looked at her. She could no sooner call him William than call the Prince Regent *Prinny*, as so many did.

"I-I will agree to Mercia," she whispered, turning her gaze back to the stage in an attempt to end the conversation.

It did not work. As Miss Darby giggled again, Mercia muttered, "My, John is on form tonight."

Charlotte knew it was best to bite her tongue, but how could she? She was the chaperone, and it was all going wrong! "You do not care that the woman you invited and are publicly courting is in intimate conversation with your brother?"

"My brother likes her and did not have the courage to speak with her at your brother's wedding. This way, he does."

Charlotte glanced over to the pair at the end. The flushed cheeks and bright eyes of John and the matching expression in Miss Darby. She smiled despite herself. "Does this make you the chaperone, Mercia?"

He grinned. "I think it does. Here's hoping I am able to catch any wicked doings, like hand-holding!"

She joined in his laughter, and her gaze met his. She was flirting. Flirting, and with the Duke of Mercia!

The laughter died in her mouth, and she turned away from him—reluctantly, for the first time—to watch the stage once more. A woman was chasing another with a bright staccato song, and she tried to focus on that and not the thrill of delight, which had overwhelmed her as she laughed with Mercia.

What a man he was. Instantly able to put her at ease, and with all the charm and none of the reserve of most gentlemen in her social circle.

"For a minute there, I saw you." Mercia had leaned even closer to her, and Charlotte moved her arm into her lap, so intense was the feeling of him. "I saw the real you, Lady Charlotte, and then you crept back into your shell."

Charlotte stiffened. She did not need this…this upstart aristocrat to speak to her in such a way! Without taking her attention from the stage, she whispered coldly, "I am here to enjoy the opera, Your Grace, and to ensure proper decorum is kept. That is the role of a chaperone."

Miss Darby burst out with raucous laughter, and there were stares and mutterings from the audience below them. One person even pointed to their box.

Mercia chuckled. "You do not seem to be doing a very good job of it."

Charlotte fixed him with a knowing smile. "This is hardly my first outing as a chaperone." Leaning forward, she said archly in a carrying voice, "Goodness, Miss Darby, did you sneeze? If you are unwell, we will have to take you back home."

She stared meaningfully at Miss Darby and the Marquess. Going silent, they shifted apart in their seats, and as John caught her eye, he had the good grace to look bashful.

Charlotte sat back and inclined her head in a mock bow. It was fortunate the end of the first act occurred at the same time, for Mercia applauded, and though she was not sure, it felt as if he was applauding her, rather than the talent on the stage.

She dropped her gaze to her lap, desperate for something else to look at. "May I see your program?"

Mercia handed it over wordlessly, but as their fingers touched, there was a moment of frisson, of heat and desire, of something uncontrolled and wild. Their gazes met again.

"Lady Charlotte," Mercia said in a strangled voice with none of the bravado from before.

She nodded, hypnotized by his touch, by his voice, but before he could speak again…

"My word, what an excellent production!" John rose and stretched. "I do not think I have ever seen such a good one. Lady Charlotte, may I beg a favor?"

Charlotte was unsure whether her voice would work, so she nodded as she busied herself with her gloves. It was the interval, and she was saved from whatever magic the duke was weaving.

John smiled nervously and glanced at Miss Darby before continuing. "Miss Darby has kindly agreed to accompany me on a carriage ride. Would…would you be so good as to join us?"

Charlotte's heart sank. For a minute, perhaps two, she had been the heroine of her story. But she had tricked herself into thinking there was a possibility of a romance between her and Mercia. Now she was back where she belonged, as the secondary character in someone else's romance.

With a smile plastered on her face, she opened her mouth to agree.

"We would love to," Mercia said smoothly.

Miss Darby beamed and leaned to speak with John more closely.

Charlotte stared at Mercia. "What exactly is your game, Your Grace? I warn you, I am no chit of the Season to be easily teased."

But were those words true? His growing smile was doing something strange to her, something she did not quite understand.

"This carriage ride is an excellent idea," he said in a low voice, "because it will give me the chance to know you better. You intrigue me, Lady Charlotte, and no other woman in Bath has managed that."

Pleasure rushed through her, but she would not let it overwhelm her. She would be the mistress of her mind and body.

"I shall be Miss Darby's chaperone," she said quietly, "not your companion."

She rose, but Mercia mirrored her, towering over her. "We'll see."

CHAPTER FOUR

"**I** TELL YOU, you are wrong!"

The glass of port slammed onto the table, and the remnants sloshed over the side. Several gentlemen who had been sitting in the club quietly, attending to newspapers or dozing in armchairs, looked up with disdain.

John laughed. "By Jove, Mercia! If you had not inherited that title after our great uncle died, you would not be permitted to shout in a club like the York!"

William grinned at his brother opposite him, a bottle of port drained to its dregs between them. They had been there almost four hours, and as the bottle emptied, their volume increased.

"Well then, it is a good thing I was the one to inherit it," William said, his smile unwavering, "for I have no intention of being quiet!"

A gentleman with a graying beard frowned and opened his mouth to speak. Before he did, his neighbor leaned over and whispered something in his ear. William heard *Duke of Mercia* muttered, and the first gentleman's eyes widened. He looked at his companion, received a nod, and looked back at William with a smirk.

William sighed. God's teeth, he had not been raised to nobility; he had not been raised to anything. A gentleman's upbringing was all he had been afforded, and it had been more than enough.

Until the letter. Now it was bowing and hierarchy and impressing people without even trying. It was bizarre, this world of pomp and circumstance, and each time he relaxed, something reminded him he was not only an outsider but one with a title that demanded respect from people he did not even know.

He shifted in his chair uncomfortably and was in half a mind to tell the gentleman with the beard that if he had a problem, he should say it rather than swallow it because of society's rules.

But no, he was a duke, and he had to act like it. Whether he wanted to or not.

"Well, I shall argue with you no more on the point," John hiccupped, putting his glass down. "I suppose it is unseemly for me to bicker with the head of my family. I just…I wish Honora was around to see us."

Something painful flamed in William's heart as though he had been punched.

Three years. Had it been that long? Yes, years had passed since he had last seen her. She could be out there in the world, hurt, worried, lost, believing he did not care about her. That she did not matter. That he had forgotten about her.

William's hands balled into fists, and a savage anger overtook him. He would burn the world down if it would bring Honora back.

"We will find her," John's words were quiet, but they interrupted William's thoughts as if they had been shouted.

"And what are we doing about it, Gloucester? Sitting here, the two of us, in our fancy gentleman's club, drinking port."

"That is not true," said John fiercely. "You know what we have done, what we have had others do on our behalf. Think of all the advertisements we have put out, the reports we have made and sent up and down the country. Think of the money and bribes we have spent gaining information, asking anyone and everyone who could have an inkling about where she is. I do believe we are doing all we can."

William shrugged, pain behind his eyes that threatened to become tears. "If it was enough, we would have found her."

What more could they do? There were few avenues they had not explored, and although money made people talk, it could not solve everything.

No one had seen their sister in three years.

"—don't you think?"

William blinked at John. "What?"

His brother laughed. "Christ alive, Mercia, I do not know what has got into you lately! I said I was sorry for keeping Miss Darby to myself at the opera. To tell the truth, I would not have pursued her if I did not believe she returned my affections. I should have discussed the matter with you first."

William shrugged. Truth be told, he had not given a single thought to Miss Darby since he had reached out and helped Lady Charlotte descend from her carriage. At that moment, all thought of the young chit still waiting in the carriage had been utterly driven from his mind.

Lady Charlotte. A puzzle. There was something about her, mysterious and whimsical, with a maturity and grace that drew him unlike any of the things fluttering fans or eyelashes.

Miss Darby? John could have her. It was Lady Charlotte he wanted to know better. She kept him awake at night. He wanted to touch her, kiss her…

William swallowed. It would not do to get carried away. Lady Charlotte was the daughter and sister of a duke, and unlike him, she had been raised with the knowledge of her place in society.

"Have Miss Darby," he said nonchalantly with a grin. "I have been introduced to more pretty young chits than I can count. You are more than welcome to my leftovers!"

John punched him good-naturedly on the arm. "Now then, William, I have no need of your leftovers! You may be the greatest womanizer of the Forty Sixths, but you have lost your touch since you left the regiment."

A lazy smile crept over William's face. "That was years ago, John, and I do not believe *greatest* is a term I appreciate, nor *womanizer!*"

"There was not a single woman in Nice who had not received some sort of affection from the dashing major," John laughed. "And most of them were hanging off your every word by the time you left. The tears, my God, I have heard tales of the weeping caused by the news you would be leaving them!"

It had certainly been surprising just how many women had been affected by his regiment's orders to return to England. William had been more than a little sorry to say goodbye to Marie, a woman he had spent time with.

"All that is past me," he said. "I am a duke now, and that requires a little more sense when deciding where to rest my head."

A grin from John was enough to make William realize how his words could be interpreted.

"You know what I mean! Besides, ladies talk here in England. You can hardly look at one without someone assuming you have professed your undying love to her, and I have no wish for the Mrs. Bryants of the world to write missives to me about my behavior."

"I have never seen so many eager beauties in one place," John said heartily. "I shall have to start being more careful and discrete. We can't have the heir to the dukedom acting in such a wild manner. No more seducing women or visiting houses of ill-repute for me!"

He chuckled, draining the bottle of port into his glass and throwing the contents into his mouth.

William grinned wryly. "That behavior is now expected of me. Dukes are meant to have mistresses, aren't they, one in each city, and one stowed away at home! As long as I marry and have plenty of sons to carry on the family name, it does not matter."

"Well, there is no need to hurry," John said in a mock-serious tone, placing his empty glass on the table. "I am sure, given time, Miss Darby can give me plenty!"

The two brothers guffawed and received several frowns from gentlemen around the room, but that did nothing to quell their merriment.

William called out to the waiter standing quietly by the door. "Another bottle here, my man!"

There was an appraising glance and then a nod from the servant, who within a minute, had brought them a second bottle of the most expensive port the York Club could offer. John attempted to open it before the waiter took pity on him and opened it for him, pouring two generous helpings of the blood-red liquid into their glasses.

"Have one yourself, why don't you," William said generously.

The servant pinked around the ears.

"Thank you, Your Grace," he said in a squeaky voice, "but I am not permitted to drink while serving the gentlemen of the club."

John chuckled. "Poor sod, off you go then."

The servant hurried back to his post, eyes averted from the brothers.

William raised his glass in a toast, but his joyful expression had disappeared, and he stared intently.

"Honestly," John said quietly. "You do not mind?"

William smiled. No matter how much his brother jested, there was a serious soul in there somewhere, and every now and again, he got a glimpse of it.

"Honestly," he said. "I do not mind. Take Miss Darby, if you can persuade her to have you. Be happy."

William thought of when he had touched Charlotte's arm, the instant their fingers had touched after he had passed her the program.

He had known women, all soldiers had. It was part of the life on campaign, and no one thought much of it—or of them. They were just women, there to perform a service.

This was new. He had never experienced anything like it before, and unless he was mistaken, neither had Charlotte.

John drained his glass once more. "You are right—Miss Darby has plenty of friends, bound to. I will ask her to invite one of them to the carriage ride."

William was startled from his stupor. "Why?"

"Why, for you, of course!" John laughed, spraying the table with port. "We cannot have you getting lonely!"

He could have blamed the port or the heat of the room. But it was because Lady Charlotte had been on his mind continuously since the opera, barely aware how it had ended, conscious she was leaving his presence, and he had not said half the things he had wanted to say to her.

These thoughts caused William to take a drink and say without thinking, "No need, Gloucester. I will have Charlotte."

A wide grin crept over John's mouth. "Oh, a new conquest! And why have I not heard of her, you sly old dog?"

William laughed. "Not heard of her? You have met her several times, you clod, and she accompanied us to the opera. Lady Charlotte. The chaperone."

"Y-you cannot be serious!" He managed to place his drink down. "I hate to scoff, Mercia, but your sense of humor is getting wild! The chaperone!"

Irritation sparked in William's heart as his brother laughed, but he did not say anything. Perhaps the second bottle of port had been a mistake.

"No, you mock me by suggesting her," John said, still grinning. "Dear God, the chaperone! Well, if it's a nursemaid you are looking for, I think you have found the perfect candidate."

He did not think. At his brother's words, William stood for a fight, fists raised, pulse pounding in his ears.

"Steady on there, Mercia!" His brother raised his hands in surrender, eyes wide.

The gentleman with the graying beard looked irritated, evidently unable to concentrate on his reading, and after folding his newspaper, walked out of the room.

William took a deep breath and tried to calm down. He was being a fool; anyone could see that. She was not his to defend, and he was an idiot for even suggesting it. He lowered himself back into his chair.

"What has got into you?"

John looked genuinely concerned, and William shook his head. "I-I won't take any rudeness about a lady, especially a St. Maur. She is nobility, born and bred into it, not like us. I will not have it."

Why was he so overwhelmed with anger? It was ridiculous, this sudden need to protect a woman who was not even here.

A vision of Lady Charlotte standing behind him as a horde of French soldiers approached them hit his mind, and he reveled in the way she clung to him.

William shook his head. It was unseemly, and what's more, a fantasy. There was no chance Lady Charlotte would consider him a suitor. She had been charmed by many a gentleman who had been born for such a thing, and she was still unmarried. Evidently, she had turned them all down.

"I will not say another word about her." John still appeared shaken by his brother's violent outburst. "I trust I am safe?"

William nodded. He had to get this obsession under control. Lady Charlotte was nothing to do with him and was merely the chaperone of his brother's conquest.

A smile crept over his face. Perhaps that was all for now. But things could change.

CHAPTER FIVE

I T WAS FIVE past eleven. There was no way to ignore it. Charlotte could see the clock over the mantelpiece from where she was seated.

Five past eleven, and they had not yet arrived.

The two Lennox brothers. She was sitting here waiting like a green girl for one of them.

Charlotte scrunched her nose and stood, pacing around the room like a cat. This was ridiculous. The last thing she wanted to do was spend another few hours as a chaperone, but it would mean William's company—and she could not decide whether that was a blessing or curse.

The memory of his hand on hers, the heat between them, a connection she did not understand, rushed through her mind, and she sat heavily on the sofa.

Is this what people felt when they were attracted to someone? Was that it, the beginnings of love, or lust, or whatever it was that encouraged two people to meet at the top of an aisle and speak vows to each other?

Charlotte pulled her pelisse tighter around her. This was nonsense, and she should put it out of her mind. The duke was certainly not thinking such things, and she would only embarrass herself. He may not be interested in Miss Darby, but he was certainly not interested in her.

Picking up her reticule, she glanced at her reflection in a small looking glass and frowned. Her bonnet was crooked.

The door opened, and Matthews entered. "The Duke of Mercia and the Marquess of Gloucester are here, my lady."

Charlotte was still frowning as she attempted to straighten her bonnet.

The butler coughed. "They have…"

"Yes, I know, thank you, Matthews," Charlotte said distractedly, giving up the bonnet as a lost cause and turning to face him with a weary smile. "Let's get this over with, shall we? I expect to be a few hours, so please ensure luncheon is on the table by half-past one, two o'clock at the latest. If I am not here by then, eat it yourself and expect me sometime in the afternoon."

The butler bowed as Charlotte swept past him, taking a deep breath to prepare herself.

As soon as she stepped into the hallway, she saw William, and the sunlight streaming through the front door accentuated his handsome features. She swallowed as she dropped into a curtsey.

Do not allow yourself to become overwhelmed, she told herself as her eyes rested on the floor. *You are a St. Maur and not that sort of woman. And you are too old!*

As she raised her head, she saw both brothers bow.

John spoke first. "How are you this morning, Lady Charlotte?"

She thought briefly of the sleepless night in anticipation of today's meeting, the hurried breakfast, and the agony of deciding which bonnet to wear.

"Very well, thank you," she said. Her eyes flicked over to the silent person in the room, willing him to speak.

But William just smiled as if perfectly aware of her wish, which he had decided to refuse.

"Shall we depart?" John gestured at the door.

She stepped past William with a spark of irritation in her heart. Why had he been so…well, attentive was the only word one could use, last week when they had gone to the opera, only to be silent now?

She saw precisely why when she saw two curricles waiting outside.

"But—but I thought we were all going to go together in a barouche?" She turned to the brothers, hoping her accusatory tone was not too obvious.

"Ah," John said, glancing at his brother. "W-well, you see, Lady Charlotte, the thing was not, exactly…"

The Duke of Mercia shrugged with a grin. "My dear Lady Charlotte, there was not a barouche to be had in Bath! We have had to settle on two curricles, and I know you will acquiesce when you see what a fine build they both have and how delicately they have been painted."

She stared. This was intolerable. What cheek! They had both known full well that a barouche where all four of them could sit together was the only acceptable transport, and here she was, completely fooled!

The duke was grinning too knowingly. Heat surged through her at the thought of sitting in a curricle with him alone, all nestled up together.

And only yesterday she had sent her own carriage back to Stonehaven Lacey. A coincidence that played right into their favor.

Finding her voice, she said stiffly, "Well, you have certainly made my role as chaperone difficult, my lord marquess, for I cannot comprehend how I can fit with yourself and Miss Darby. Unless you are suggesting, the best chaperoning occurs from a distance of ten feet in a completely different curricle?"

John had the good grace to look sheepish as he clasped his hands behind his back. "I had thought of that, Lady Charlotte, and as Miss Darby and I will be in the front, we will always be within view to ensure nothing untoward is happening."

Charlotte glared at him. They had been clever and forced her into a corner. What could she do? Her own carriage was miles away by now, and it would not do for a duke, a marquess, and a St. Maur to hire a common hackney.

What could she say? Either announce she did not think it a good idea, thus silently accusing John of ill intentions, cancel the day entirely, or...

Miss Darby would never forgive her if she canceled her time with the Marquess of Gloucester.

What's more, and this thought caused Charlotte to stand up straighter, *her St. Maur name was well-respected in Bath, and if she declined to chaperone him, John would struggle to find anyone else. His reputation amongst the mamas of society would be ruined, and that would, in turn, ruin his chances of marriage this Season, if not longer.*

Charlotte twisted her fingers around her reticle. There was no choice in the matter, and she had almost resolved to allow it with a short, sharp word with John later about taking advantage of her good nature when her eyes fell on William.

John was watching her innocently, hopeful but concerned he had gone too far.

Not so with his brother. She stepped back at the hunger on William's face, his eyes filled with such intensity, she had to move. He was staring so desperately; he might convince her of anything.

"What do you say, Charlotte?" His gaze did not waver from hers.

Charlotte's jaw dropped. Only one person alive called her Charlotte, and her brother called her Lotty most of the time. It was astonishing to hear her name spoken with such little respect—and astonishing to feel exhilaration rush through her body.

A shaky smile crept over her face. "We must not keep Miss Darby waiting."

John grinned. "Oh, thank you, Lady Charlotte. I am entirely in your debt, as you well know."

She relaxed as she saw his genuine pleasure. "I do. Do not ask me to stick my neck out for you again, do you hear?"

The younger brother grinned, and he rushed over to the first curricle, leaving Charlotte alone with William.

The duke offered his hand. "Let me assist you into the curricle, my lady."

Her hesitation was brief. She did not want to place her hand in his. What if she felt the same heat, the same magnetism, which she could not explain?

Without waiting for a response, he took her hand and led her to the curricle. Within seconds, Charlotte found herself seated beside him, her hip pressed against his leg. Her heart pounded, and the pelisse she had chosen was suddenly too hot. How could she endure an entire curricle ride with him?

The first curricle moved off, and the duke clicked his tongue, encouraging their horses to follow. Charlotte had expected him to speak and had a few forceful putdowns ready. But he said nothing.

Eventually, the silence became oppressive. As they passed people on the pavement, they looked with surprise to see her in the company of a gentleman, which did nothing for her own peace of mind. This was intolerable; he had to say something!

"Ah, and there is Miss Darby."

Charlotte looked over where the duke was pointing. Miss Darby, wearing a turban of the height of fashion, was waiting, unbridled excitement splashed across her features.

Charlotte smiled. There was truly no guile in Miss Darby, no need to guess her affections, and if John could be relied upon to speak when necessary, she had the feeling her chaperoning duties would soon be over.

It took Miss Darby no time to be helped into the curricle beside John, and they set off into the bustle of Bath at a gentle pace.

John must have said something, for Miss Darby threw back her head and laughed.

Charlotte swallowed. "I must say, Your Grace, I…"

"William." He gave her a wry smile. "I think a duke and the daughter of a duke can have a more relaxed approach to names. After all, I call you Charlotte."

"You should call me Lady Charlotte," she corrected, her hands clasped in her lap and face resolutely facing forward, watching the other curricle.

"Not always."

"You do know the rules of propriety dictate I should address you with nothing but *Your Grace* when I am with you, and the *Duke of Mercia* when I am not?"

"And? Do you think I have lived by the rules all my life? You know my history, Charlotte. I have had this millstone of a title a few years. Why not call me what my mother chose for me? Besides, I like the name William. Don't you?"

It was overwhelmingly hot in the curricle, but Charlotte had no way of rearranging herself, so she was not pushed close against him. Besides, it was rather intoxicating, the thought of calling this man by his first name. As though he was not a duke. As though he had no power over her.

She swallowed. This went against everything she had been taught. Obligation forced her to speak. "Fine. William, I must apologize you are not with Miss Darby, or another young, pretty thing. I am sure that was who this curricle was intended for."

William shrugged. "To be frank, I would rather be with you."

She snorted and covered her mouth with her hand.

Her companion laughed as they turned the corner to Milsom Street. "You do not believe me. Why not?"

"I am past my prime," she responded without any hint of self-compassion. "It is clear my time as the giggling girl in the first curricle is over, though to tell the truth, I did not experience it much. No, at my time of life, it is right and proper to be the chaperone, and I am happy to be."

It was probably the least bitter speech she had ever made about her chaperoning life, and Charlotte was pleased to have managed it.

But William was evidently unconvinced. "Are you?"

"Am I what?"

"Happy to be a chaperone," he said baldly, beholding her with those fierce eyes.

Charlotte's fingers fidgeted. How was it possible that this gentleman could pull the truth from her? "Not particularly, no."

He snorted, and she could not help but look up. "Then why in God's name do it? You are more than capable of catching the attention of a gentleman, after all. You are doing it right now."

Was it possible to be any hotter?

She cleared her throat. "I do not want to discuss this with anyone."

"No, you do not," he said, far more serious. "But if not with me, then who else? I am neither brother nor intimate, and I will not judge you nor laugh at you."

She hesitated. It was tempting to pour her heart out, but how could she trust him? She barely knew him. What if her words found their way into the gossip pages of the local rag?

She forced her fingers to stop moving. If not now, then when? If not him, then who?

"It feels…" She coughed but continued as William smiled. "It feels as though I am being left behind."

He shrugged. "I do not see how."

"Well, of course, you don't, you are a gentleman!" she snapped, temper rising. "Gentlemen marry at any age, and there is no comment on it whatsoever. But for ladies… most of my peers have children of their own nearing fourteen, and in a few years, they themselves will be eligible for a match."

"And that bothers you?"

She hesitated again. It was madness to be revealing her deepest thoughts to this gentleman, and in an open curricle, too! But there was something about him. Something made her trust him.

"More so with each passing year. You see other people fall in love.

43

They meet someone they have never known before, and all of a sudden, the rest of the world doesn't matter anymore, only each other," she said wistfully. "They find their perfect partner, the one person who they can spend their life with. And then there's me."

William watched her, but Charlotte found she did not feel embarrassed. Then he nodded sagely. "Truth be told, I am informed my title needs another heir—poor John isn't sufficient—and I had resigned myself to it and carried out those required steps to meet with the ladies of society. But since I have found you, that search has been…intolerable."

Heat rushed to Charlotte's cheeks as she blustered, "Come now, Your Grace—William. You cannot be serious."

Surely, he could not, for who would even consider her as a potential mother at her age? She tried not to look at him as they sped down a slope, hoping the breeze would cool her face.

"Why not?"

Before she knew it, a hand was placed on her thigh. It seared her skin as though his touch was a brand, as though he was marking her for his own. She gasped at the intensity of the sensation.

"What you have forgotten, Charlotte," William said in a low voice, dripping with desire, "is though you are acting as a chaperone for Miss Darby, no one is acting as a chaperone for you."

Impossible to think clearly, she tried to ignore the weight of his fingers curled around her thigh in that delightful way.

"I do not need a chaperone—oh!"

She had only managed to say a few words before she was overcome as William lightly stroked her inner leg. Her whole body was on fire, the flames starting wherever his fingers touched. Even through the material of her gown, every caress seared.

Charlotte breathed, "You cannot do that."

William's other hand was still guiding the horses, and he was able to manage them while touching her in such a wonderful, terrible way.

He chuckled. "You can stop me anytime you wish, Charlotte. You have hands. Stop me if you don't like it."

But she was glorying in this feeling, shivering under his touch, and she wanted it to continue—and yet she had to stop him, this was too wild, too rebellious!

With a great effort of will, her hand met his with the intention of moving it, but he was stronger than she was—or perhaps she did not wish him to stop.

Charlotte moaned aloud as he continued to explore her leg with gentle strokes, unable to restrain herself, unable to slow the beating of her heart.

"William," she whispered, unsure what she was going to say next.

"William, we have to turn back!"

Charlotte jolted at the sound and saw John leaning back in his curricle.

"Why?" William called, his hand still placed heavily on her thigh.

"It looks like rain, and these curricles are no match for strong wind," John called back. "We cannot have Miss Darby and Lady Charlotte drenched through. We will have to return them home."

Charlotte was still catching her breath as William turned to her and whispered, "I think I would quite like you wet, Charlotte. What do you say?" Without waiting for her response, he shouted back to his brother, "Fine by me, John, lead the way."

As the curricles turned right at the next opportunity, William removed his hand to steer the horses.

"I-I do not know," she said shakily, "how you have the audacity to...to touch me like that."

"I wanted to touch you like that," William shot back. "I have wanted to touch you since I saw you seated on that piano stool. If anything, I think I should be applauded for waiting so long."

She spluttered, unsure what to say.

"More importantly," he said with a wicked smile, "don't you want to be touched?"

She stared open-mouthed, and his grin broadened. How could he possibly know what pleasure his fingers gave her, how alive her body had felt in those moments, more alive than any other time in her life.

"Now then, before I return you to the safety of your home," William said, all intensity gone, "I have an invitation to make to you. I am attending Braedon's ball tomorrow, and I would like you to accompany me."

Charlotte sagged in the curricle, relieved to return to normality. Rain started to drizzle down, causing shrieks from young ladies on the pavement, their hands reaching for their bonnets. "Of course. Who will I be chaperoning?"

A frown creased his forehead. "No one. I am inviting you as my guest."

It was the last response she had expected. Invited as his guest? She could not remember the last time that had happened.

She imagined entering a room filled with candles and noisy guests who fell silent at the sight of her on the arm of such a handsome man. Even in her mind, someone pointed at her and laughed. There was chatter from a corner and a snort, which was shushed.

Charlotte stiffened as the curricle pulled up outside her home. It was pouring with rain now; John had been correct in his guess at the changing weather.

She would not make a laughingstock of herself and could not attend a ball with someone who made her feel things she could not explain.

"No, thank you," she said abruptly.

Opening the door to the curricle, she did not wait for William to descend and help her down. The front door was already being opened by Matthews, and she almost made it inside without another word from the handsome duke.

"Charlotte."

Just her name was enough to make her stop and turn around. How did he have such power over her?

He was still seated in the curricle, and there was a look of disappointment across on his face.

"You do know your refusal makes me even more determined to win you, don't you?" He grinned as his gaze flickered over her body. Laughing, he pulled away, shouting behind him, "Until the ball!"

CHAPTER SIX

WILLIAM BOWED AND hoped to God the boring young woman before him had not noticed his stifled yawn.

"…which was what I said to her, yet she clearly had not listened, for when I saw her today…"

Was this ball never-ending? He had been forced to accept the invitation, as he always had since taking this godforsaken title.

How much easier things were when he had been Major Lennox. If he had not wished to attend a ball, he had not. If he did not wish to speak to a person or listen to them drone on about something which did not capture his interest, he could mutter an apology and leave.

But now he was a duke, always on the edge of offending someone by not laughing at the right time, or nodding after a certain phrase, or praising a particular person. It was intolerable, this continuous need to keep society happy.

"…for the mistake was entirely his own, and he did understand this when I pointed it out…"

Another yawn was forced down as William's eyes glazed. He was trapped in conversation with a young woman who may have been Miss Jones or Miss Jane, he could not remember which, and her mother.

If he had known how utterly dull this ball was going to be, he would not have come. Or at least he would have spent more than five seconds attempting to construct an excuse. Perhaps he should have done so the moment Lady Charlotte rejected him.

The memory of stroking her thigh in the curricle as she quivered under his touch sparked in his mind. A wicked grin crept over his face.

It was the slightest of touches. His manhood throbbed painfully at the thought of being the first man to make Charlotte cry out with ecstasy, those dark lashes fluttering.

"...do not you think?"

Miss Jones stared. Uncomfortably jolted back to the present, William opened his mouth with little thought of what he would say.

"I am sure, Your Grace agrees," said the mother. She was smiling indulgently at her daughter as though she was the most incredible thing she had ever seen.

William tried not to sigh. Was it possible to have an interesting conversation at all? Bath was absolutely packed full of people, but the only person who had spoken any sense to him since he had arrived was Charlotte.

"I do indeed agree," he said hastily.

Miss Jones looked delighted, a delicate flush gracing her cheeks. Her mother looked between the two of them with a satisfied nod.

"Come, Jane," she said. "We must not monopolize His Grace's time. If we stay talking with him much longer, there will be gossip about the two of you!"

Mother and daughter dropped into low curtseys, Miss Jones tilting her shoulders to allow him a deeper look down her gown, and they were gone.

William blew out a breath. What a harridan! And yet, she had been no different, truth be told, than half a dozen of the other young ladies who had moved toward him as though stalking him in the wild.

His gaze fell on the dancers, watching them lazily. He had always heard such good reports of Braedon's balls, but this one was the slowest he had ever attended.

He was no fool. Painful as it was to admit, if Charlotte—Lady

Charlotte, he must call her that in company—had agreed to accompany him, he would have enjoyed the evening.

The moment she had refused him, he had been plagued with twin feelings of frustration and longing. How could she deny him after tantalizing her so? How could he find so little joy here because one woman was absent?

How strange that she could have such power over him so quickly.

The music ended, and the dancers bowed and curtseyed, moving away to their respective parties, leaving him a clear view of Charlotte seated on the other side of the room.

William's breath caught in his throat. So, she had rejected him but attended anyway—the minx! Her blue gown looked worn, washed so frequently it had become gray, and she was wearing no jewels or feathers of any kind.

None of this prevented her from being the most beautiful woman in the room.

Something jolted in his stomach, and William unconsciously brought his hand up as though he had been physically punched. It wasn't lust, but it was damn close.

She was speaking to a young woman and had not noticed him at all. Excitement flared as he began to stride across the ballroom floor.

"Your Grace, this is a fine meeting!" Miss Emma Tilbury greeted him with a wicked smile, one which had already felled a duke or two, but William had not taken his eyes from Charlotte. She looked up, saw him coming, and flushed. With embarrassment? With pleasure?

It did not matter. She had seen him and reacted.

Before he reached her, Charlotte rose elegantly. It was not until then that he realized his heart was pounding.

"Charlotte," he said breathlessly, cursing himself silently for sounding like a fool.

"Your Grace, have you had the pleasure of being introduced to Lady Letitia Cavendish?"

She extended her hand gracefully to indicate the woman who had been seated beside her, who had jumped to her feet, pink with embarrassment.

William blinked. This had not been the conversation he had expected, and though blindsided by the introduction, he was not fool enough to miss the name. Lady Letitia Cavendish. A relation of the Duke of Devonshire, then.

He sighed. Decorum, propriety, elegance. All that was expected of him now, as a member of this elite club, which seemed to create rules for the simple pleasure of enforcing them.

"It is a pleasure to make your acquaintance, Your Grace." Lady Letitia curtsied awkwardly, evidently unsure where to look.

William's face softened. The poor girl was crippled with shyness, that much was evident. This ball was probably more of a punishment than a pleasure.

He bowed low and smiled. "Lady Letitia. What an honor to make your acquaintance. Lady Charlotte, I have come here expressly to ask you to dance. What say you?"

He had thought, foolishly, she would not refuse him in public and certainly not before her friend.

"No, thank you, Your Grace," she said quietly, her eyes unwavering. "I have no wish to dance this evening. Besides, I am accompanying Lady Letitia and have no wish to leave her side."

The flush tinging her cheeks did nothing to soften the irritation in William. This was a new experience for him: a refusal.

When a major, women were interested in him because of his uniform but would not consider him a serious suitor. He may have bedded them, but he had not bothered to pursue them. After he was made Duke of Mercia, ladies became far more interested in his person.

But Lady Charlotte was different. She was not impressed. So, what would tip the scales for her, deeds?

"You forget, Lady Charlotte," he said carefully. "I am a soldier. I am used to waiting out the enemy."

"I am well stocked for a siege," she countered. "Perhaps you had better rethink your tactics."

"I know no other." William grinned. "And I am more than willing to stick by your side the entire evening, to track you, waiting for the right moment to strike. Are you ready to spend the entirety of the night with me at your side?"

She smiled and looked at him intently. William found his breath stuck in his throat until she replied quietly, "Well then. To avoid a war, I had better surrender."

His grin widened. Could she be thinking of their encounter in the curricle?

"Lady Letitia, may I introduce you to Mrs. Coulson?" Charlotte was saying to her charge, deftly handing her responsibility as chaperone over to a matronly woman who nodded sagely. "Mrs. Coulson, Lady Letitia Cavendish."

The older woman moved to take Charlotte's place beside the younger lady. He watched the transition with his heart thumping. Even in the midst of her own story, she ensured her duty was performed.

Her fingers were warm on his hand as he led her to the dance floor to join the set. Or was that his own hand pulsating with heat? It was impossible to tell. All William knew was that his heart was thumping wildly because of her.

That changed as he noticed with surprise that people were openly pointing. One of them laughed, and an unpleasant snicker echoed around the room.

William glanced at Charlotte. Her eyes were downcast, and her cheeks were pale as her shoulders slumped.

It was not difficult to guess the cause of her upset, and as William placed her in the set, he said in a low voice, "Ignore them." The music began before he could say any more, and as he moved forward with the gentlemen in a row, he repeated, "Ignore them, Charlotte."

Forced to step back with the others as part of the dance before she was able to reply, Charlotte held her head up high and focused on him.

How could anyone look at her and not see her worth? How could they look and laugh?

The ladies stepped forward, and he said quietly, "You are the most beautiful woman in this room, Charlotte."

She blushed as she stepped away. "In this old gown?"

"You wear it to disappear, to ensure no attention falls on you," he countered, trying to ignore the thrill of holding her hand. "Otherwise, you would outshine them all."

"Outshine? Lady Charlotte?" The gentleman who they were circling with snorted. "No offense, Lady Charlotte, but as a chaperone, you do a good job of allowing the young ladies to shine. No one wants a pretty chaperone, do they?"

She stopped in her tracks, and the other lady walked into her. She was staring at William so fiercely, he thought he might burst into flames. Without saying a word, Charlotte released the hands of those on either side of her and marched away.

God's teeth! William cursed, standing and staring after her. She must have known she would attract such attention if she stood up to dance, and he had encouraged her to expose herself to such degrading comments.

"You, sir, are fortunate I do not have the time to call you out," he growled, "for you are a fool and a brigand, and I give you fair warning. You are not welcome at any event I attend in the future."

"But Your Grace, I said naught to you!" The idiot blustered, and William fought down the need to punch him. Charlotte needed him. She was far more important than teaching this cur a lesson.

Ignoring the startled cries around him, William pushed past them and toward the doorway. There were several people milling about in the hallway, some of them taking off their cloaks, a few whispering in surprise, but no Charlotte.

There was nowhere else she could have gone but outside. William nodded to the footman, who opened the door for him.

Evidently forcing back tears as she walked slowly along, was Charlotte.

"Going home, sir?" A carriage driver was smoking a pipe.

William ignored him. "Lady Charlotte, where are you going?"

She made no sign she had heard him, and he rushed to catch her. "Charlotte," he said gently as he placed a hand on her arm.

She pulled away and glared. "I am going home. Please leave me, Your Grace. I know the way. Mrs. Coulson will take care of Lady Letitia. Good evening."

William laughed darkly. "If you think I am going to allow you to walk home on your own…"

"You are not my guardian, father, brother, nor friend," she said fiercely. "You have no right to an opinion. Please, go away."

William kept pace with her.

"Bath is perfectly safe," Charlotte said angrily, "and the night air will do me good."

Her last words were said in desperation, and her tone so exactly like Honora's, that William was overwhelmed with a savage need to protect her.

"I will never allow a woman to walk home on her own again, and you may as well get accustomed to the idea, Charlotte. Never."

Although Charlotte did not stop walking, she finally looked at him. "You sound as though you have done that once before."

William swallowed. This was not what he had expected tonight. His plans had been more, well, romantic. He had been determined to woo this rigid chaperone. He had not expected this to be a night of confessions. He had never told a lady the story before.

"This is not a tale I planned to tell," he said gruffly as they turned a corner. "But if I must, I am glad it is to you, Charlotte."

"I am not asking for your confidence," she said swiftly.

William smiled sadly. "I know. But perhaps it is a story you need to hear."

He took a deep breath. Just the idea of thinking about that night all those years ago was painful. But this woman needed to know.

"I had—have—a sister named Honora. She was ten years younger than me, and we were inseparable as children—John, too. She was wild and despised rules. We loved her."

He glanced at Charlotte, who smiled. "I had two brothers, too."

William nodded. "As I grew older, I needed a profession, and as the eldest son, my parents used what little money they had to buy me a commission in the army. I did well, and with the money I managed to put aside, I dedicated myself to advancement. After notes in dispatches of valor and bravery, I was promoted. With the greater income, I was finally able to support my family. I purchased a commission for John. Soon to become Major Lennox, I came back to London for a visit, and the three of us were invited to a ball."

A laughing couple passed them, and William stepped closer to Charlotte. He could feel her like fire—hot and tempting.

He coughed. "John was unwell, recovering from a bout of influenza, so Honora and I went together. It was a rather dull affair for my sister, with few gentlemen, but I ran into some friends from my previous regiment. Honora grew tired and wanted to go home, and I was having the time of my life."

His words stuck in his throat.

"And so," Charlotte prompted gently, "she walked home on her own."

"It was selfish of me," he said fiercely. "I was far more interested in my own enjoyment, and we were but two streets away from the rooms we had taken. How difficult could it be, I thought, for her to walk two streets? Before I could tell her to be careful, she had already gone."

They walked for a minute in complete silence before he continued.

"That was the last time I saw her." His voice cracked as he knew it would, but the guilt was impossible to ignore. "Honora never made it home. She has been missing from that day, and it has been three painful years, and we are still no closer to knowing what befell my sister that night."

They crossed the street and only then was the silence broken.

"That is awful," Charlotte whispered. "I had no idea, William. No idea at all."

He breathed out the tension in his shoulders. "Well, it is hardly polite dinner conversation. Even now, I still enter every room in the hope someone will turn around and it will be Honora."

There, he had trusted her with his darkest secret, his deepest fear, and hope.

He had expected Charlotte to shy away, to chastise him for such reckless care of his sister.

She did neither of those things. Instead, she took his hand and slipped her fingers between his. "There was nothing you could have done, William," she said quietly. "You could never have predicted it."

William squeezed her hand, not trusting his voice, but feeling a new closeness with her.

But he could not wallow in self-pity; he did not deserve it. "I have heard the murmurs of course, the gossips wondering whether anyone in the family had something to do with it. But the very idea someone could hurt her!" Bitterness seeped into every word.

"They always know exactly how to hurt you," Charlotte said quietly, and as he glanced at her, she smiled. "That is why gossips have such power, and the best way to break that power is to ignore them or remove yourself from the situation. Why do you think I ran out of the ball tonight?"

She stopped suddenly, and William was pulled toward her, their hands still joined.

"Why have you stopped walking, Charlotte?"

"Because this is my house."

What a fool for not noticing! He had been so lost in his words, pouring out his soul to her, he had forgotten where they were.

He chuckled. "Thank you for listening to me."

"Thank you for seeing me safely home."

William swallowed. With any other lady, he would simply kiss her. Take her in his arms and show her, not tell her, how he felt.

But this was Charlotte. She was already more important than any other woman he had ever met. He did not want to get this wrong. He had one opportunity to show her exactly what she meant to him.

"I have not got you home safely yet," he said and pulled her up the steps, toward the front door.

"You can consider your duty performed."

"Nothing with you is a duty, Charlotte." He had not meant his words to be serious, but with such a tantalizing woman before him, it was impossible for them not to be. Without thinking, just feeling, he leaned her against the door. The gasp that escaped her lips pushed him over the edge, and he crushed his lips on hers.

Charlotte resisted at first, but as William brought his arms around her, she softened in his hold, deepening the kiss by allowing her lips to slowly part.

It was even more glorious than he could have thought. Everything about her drew him in, so fragile and so strong. She moved against him, moaning. And in response, he groaned, wanting to seduce her.

But no. If he was going to do this, he would do it properly.

He broke the kiss but did not permit her to move away from the door.

"I think," Charlotte said breathlessly, not looking away, "that I may need a chaperone of my own after all."

William laughed shakily. "I am determined, Charlotte. I will marry you."

Her eyes widened, and her lips parted in astonishment. "Marry me?"

He nodded. "God's teeth, Charlotte, you do such things to me... I think I may actually marry you."

She blinked rapidly, staring unbelieving at him. "No, William."

Her hand had found the door handle, and she opened it, slipping inside and closing it swiftly behind her.

William turned, breathing heavily, gazing at the deserted street. What a magnificent woman. He would make her beg for him, his touch, and his name—before the month was out.

CHAPTER SEVEN

I T WAS A struggle to keep a smile on her face as Charlotte came to the end of another circuit at the Pump Room. Every day during the Season, especially when the weather was unfavorable, people would come here to see and be seen. She was a St. Maur, so of course, she was here.

She inclined her head in response to someone's curtsey but did not pause to talk. It was impossible; the room was so full and the slow but steady movement of the crowd so continuous, she was swept away.

The whole of Bath was here, and though Charlotte recognized many faces, there was not a single person she wished to converse with. Her thoughts were so rapid, she needed to untangle them first.

"Your Grace, or can I call you William?"

Charlotte looked over to the other side of the room and saw him.

He was well hidden by a screen of young ladies, all standing around him with beaming smiles and wide eyes.

A smile crept across Charlotte's face as she continued to promenade around the room. Poor William. It was a curse really, to be so handsome and so eligible. He probably hadn't got a word in edgeways with those ladies.

No sooner did the thought cross her mind, did she regret it and scold herself for such an opinion.

Why should she criticize or condemn other women—especially women she did not even know—because they happened to be smiling

MILY E K MURDOCH

at a man she…

How did she feel about him?

Her mind jumped back to that heady kiss, three days ago. Her back against her front door, his arms around her, and his lips…

Charlotte bumped into an elderly gentleman who looked severely affronted.

"Mind where you are going, Lady Charlotte," he said crossly, a deep frown across his forehead. "'Bad enough these misses pay no heed to their elders!'"

"My apologies, my lord," she said hastily, but he had already shuffled off.

Yes, it was easy to see how quickly people could fall in love after a kiss like that. True, she ought to have restrained herself as a lady of good breeding, but she had not wanted to. She wanted to kiss William and be kissed by him all over.

Her smile disappeared as a flush crept up her neck.

"Your brother, the Marquess, is he not here?"

A plaintive voice rose above the chatter, and she saw, to her surprise, that the circuit of the room had brought her close to William and the girls. One of them was pouting, but instead of being captivated, William caught Charlotte's gaze.

He rolled his eyes and grinned before he replied.

Charlotte was forced to look away as she laughed. There was something about that man, something playful and yet so serious.

What a jest between them! He would not seriously make her an offer, not to the chaperone. He jokingly asked to marry her, and she just as jokingly refused.

But what if he had not been in jest?

It was not possible a man like him, a man at all, would offer her marriage. No one ever had. No one considered her true marriage material. If she was honest, she had never considered herself that way either.

"If she had any decency, she would leave Bath," said a stout woman to her companion. "Throwing her heels in the air like that, what does she think she's doing?"

"I heard Miss Tilbury cares not for such rules," revealed her companion with a shocked look. "And when I spoke to…"

Their voices died away as Charlotte progressed on, and their gossip about the Earl of Marnmouth's mistress was not enough to distract her.

Marriage. Though she craved it and longed to be loved and wanted in such a way, marriage frightened her.

To be so wholly devoted to another person, to never do anything without them, it scared her. Overwhelming. Engulfing.

Reaching the opposite wall again, Charlotte turned carefully, ensuring she did not bump into anyone, and looked back across the room. Though she could no longer hear their conversations, William was still surrounded by the same girls. One of them threw her head back and laughed.

Something strange stirred in her. It was a new emotion, part determination to prove herself, part heady desire to be the one everyone looked at.

She didn't want anyone else to laugh at William's jokes. This was not like her, this impulse to put herself forward—but if she did not, she would never know whether she could.

She took a deep breath. Her corset was too tight, it seemed so recently. She would have to remember to tell Danvers.

Ignoring tradition, Charlotte broke from the pack and started to stride directly toward William.

Those she passed gasped or moved hurriedly out of the way, and a few muttered, and she caught the words *strange* and *so unlike her.* She ignored them all.

William's admirers turned, open-mouthed, to stare. William grinned, one hand in his pocket, but did not say a word.

Charlotte swallowed. Well, she had come this far. "You will not mind if I borrow him, will you?"

Without waiting for a response, she grabbed William's hand and pulled him toward the doors.

Now the gasps were more audible, and someone behind her laughed. Miss Theodosia Ashbrooke was close by and actually pointed them out to her companion, and the footman on the door gaped.

What did she care for the opinions of people she did not even like? In that moment, when an unknown gentleman had been so discourteous at Braedon's ball, she had fled—but why should she bow to society's rules at every turn? She was sick of the stuffiness of the Pump Room, sick of the formality of it all. She had to get out of there, and she wanted him with her.

She did not think until they stepped outside, and suddenly all the movement in her legs stopped. William looked delighted.

"Well, Lady Charlotte, what was all that about?"

She felt giddy and had forgotten to take a full breath. "Did you not give me the signal?" she asked airily, not attempting to hide her smile.

William's brow furrowed, and she appreciated his handsomeness. "The signal?"

She nodded. "To rescue you from all of those girls?"

The street was deserted. Rain seemed to be keeping everyone inside. William smiled and stepped closer, closer than was proper—but then who was there to see?

"I did not even think to," he said, taking her hand. "But I must say, I wish I had done so much earlier so I could escape their company and enjoy yours. Shall we?"

He indicated the pavement, and Charlotte hesitated. In all her wild excitement, she had not thought this far. All she had wanted to do was remove him from those chittering girls, and she had done so.

But now she had William to herself, and it was impossible to leave his company. She had longed for it, truth be told, for three days.

She nodded. As they walked leisurely out of the Abbey Courtyard to Stall Street, she spotted a few people who had left the Pump Room to stare. She tried, unsuccessfully, to ignore them.

"I hope I did not truly interrupt an important conversation," she said quietly.

He shook his head. "Just another discussion on the weddings they were attending, what bonnets they had chosen, whether ribbons should be wide or narrow this Season…nothing of import."

She smiled. "I am afraid I have no conversation on the subject of ribbons."

"Thank God," he said with a grin. "But you may pick up their topic of weddings, if you wish to give me a sense of continuity. Tell me, what weddings are you to attend this year?"

Charlotte shivered in the cold of the morning and tightened her grip around his arm. Of course, the topic was weddings.

"None," she said. "Which is a relief. I have no comprehension of what marriage looks like—a good marriage, I mean. It is always a rather bizarre experience, hearing two people make such extravagant vows. Besides, I have attended two already this year."

"But your parents, they must have been a model for marriage."

Charlotte laughed. "Oh, yes, a very merry couple. They were so unhappy together, and my father such a monster…"

"What do you mean, a monster?"

She swallowed. He had been so honest about his sister—and was her story any worse?

He saw her hesitation. "Please, I must apologize. I have no wish to bring up bad memories, Charlotte."

His use of her name shifted her heart. "No, it is only that he used to…to beat us. All of us."

William's eyes widened in horror. "Your brothers?"

Charlotte nodded. "And my mother and I, if we were disobedient. He was terrible when he drank, and as we grew older, he drank more."

William stopped walking. Disgust darkened his features. "You *and* your mother?"

He did not seem to believe her or didn't want to. "Please, do not concern yourself. It all changed three years ago."

"What changed his mind?"

"He died."

They stood without moving in the middle of the street as a carriage rumbled by them.

Finally, William spoke. "That is the most despicable thing I have ever heard."

Charlotte frowned and started walking with him, arm in arm. "When you grow up under such circumstances, and your father is a duke, no one questions his authority or his character. Even if they knew it was happening."

"I would never," growled William, "never permit such a man in my sight if I knew that of him."

He growled, and she appreciated his protective reaction.

"So, have you decided yet?"

The frown on William's face disappeared. "Decided what?"

"Why, which of the young ladies of Bath you are going to marry?" she said brightly.

She had intended her remark to lighten their conversation. She could not have been more wrong.

Instead of answering, William pulled her down Bilbury Lane and pushed her against the wall of the closest building.

"Going to marry?" he breathed with a wicked smile on his face. "I know exactly who I want to marry."

They were completely alone, and no one from the street could see them.

"Who have you chosen?"

William groaned and dipped his head, so his forehead touched hers. "Don't tease me, Charlotte."

The kiss began before she could speak, and it was not the restrained kiss from three days ago, but passionate. His tongue teased her lips open, and she welcomed him.

William's hands crept around her neck, drawing her closer. The kiss deepened, and she arched into him, but he pushed her roughly back against the wall, breaking the kiss and staring at her with wild eyes.

"Damn it, Charlotte," he panted. "I have wanted this—wanted you—for too long now."

She did not need his words; she wanted his touch. Wild thoughts fluttered in her mind as she lost herself in their embrace.

William's hand moved from her neck down her body, tantalizingly close to her breasts but moving to her leg. It seared her when he had touched her in the curricle, and once again, there was nothing innocent about the way he caressed her.

He started to push up her skirts, and she gasped at the sudden rush of longing she felt but did not understand.

"Is that you, Bert?" a man's voice echoed down the alleyway.

William broke the kiss and immediately covered her with his body to protect her from being seen.

"Bert?" The man shouted again, the echo bouncing off the walls.

Charlotte could feel William's heart pounding. It mirrored her own as she felt his hardness throbbing against her.

Without someone answering him, the gentlemen moved away, his shadow disappearing from the end of the lane.

"You are lucky," William said in a low voice.

Charlotte swallowed nervously. "How so?"

He nodded. "Lucky I am able to control myself. Does this mean you are seriously considering marrying me?"

She could not speak. Her mind was awash with images of what would have happened if that stranger had not attempted to find his friend.

The word *yes* was on her tongue, but it was all too quick. Her mind might be ready for him, but was her heart? Was this just a game to him?

She needed time to think—time away from William's intoxicating presence.

"No," she whispered.

William staggered away as though burned. "No?"

Charlotte hated the disappointment on his face, but surely this was better than blindly accepting? She had been a chaperone for too long to be ignorant of the dangers of rash proposals and blind acceptance. Could she trust a man she barely knew? Was this not just a joke between them?

"No," she repeated breathlessly. "William…"

"God's teeth, woman," he muttered ruefully, his eyes never leaving hers. "Every taste of you makes me want you more. I cannot take this much longer."

Without another word, he stepped away, leaving Charlotte alone, leaning against the brick wall and feeling more alive than ever before.

"Come now," he said, gaze finally dropped to the ground. "I should return you home. This is no place for a lady."

She attempted to gain her breath. A lady? She had never felt less like one than in this moment.

"Do…do we have to leave this minute?"

The words had escaped before she had been able to consider them, but William's smile was enough to assure her she had not spoken out of turn.

He pulled her into his arms and pressed his lips against hers, and Charlotte lost herself in the heady world of his embrace.

CHAPTER EIGHT

WILLIAM GROANED. THE sharp light that could only mean morning was piercing through the curtains in his rented room. He had never believed it possible to wake up on the wrong side of the bed, but his throbbing headache increased as he opened his eyes.

Today was a day for staying in bed and doing absolutely nothing.

"Wake up, lazybones!" John's voice echoed down the corridor, and William raised a hand to his head. "It is almost nine in the morning, and the day is almost gone."

A clattering noise told William his brother had moved to the third room they occupied, where they ate and entertained the few guests of their acquaintance in Bath.

He groaned as he sat up, head spinning. After such an intense meeting with Charlotte two—or was it three days ago?—he had been bored out of his mind ever since. Who could compare to her? What conversation would enthrall him?

William finally stood with ill grace and pulled on his trousers, a shirt, and the waistcoat that was nearest.

He was met with ill-humor when he entered the room where John waited.

"Why do you look as though you've lost all your money on the horses?" John asked grumpily, barely looking up from his newspaper.

William bit back the retort that he was in a better mood than John seemed to me. "Anything interesting?"

John rustled the pages but did not look up. "Plenty of nonsense about the Season, and what everyone is wearing. Can you think of anything duller?"

He could but did not consider now the best time to say so. Instead, William dropped into the only other chair at the table and looked, a little disconsolately, at the breakfast provided by their landlord.

A few potatoes, more burnt than baked, a loaf of bread that was older than most the chits at the Pump Room, and a flagon of something that was probably ale.

William curled his lips in distaste. "We need to get a footman, a manservant, something. It is disgraceful that the Duke of Mercia has to eat like this."

"Hark at you!" John said irritably. "This fare was good enough for you when you were Major Lennox. Does nobility affect one's tastes as well as one's pocket?"

He had never been good at hiding his emotions from his younger brother. William swallowed down his second bitter retort of the morning.

John was seated awkwardly, hunched as though he could not bear to sit upright. His ears were red, and he huffed as he turned another page.

William sighed. "What is the matter, John? You surely have nothing to complain about. Something is bothering you, and I would much rather know now than endure this temper all day."

The newspaper was dropped. "I will tell you, if you are that concerned about me," he said with a frown. "Not that you have noticed until now."

But his words were interrupted by a loud knock on the door, which opened before either brother could respond. Their landlord stood there, short and stocky, with two envelopes in his coal-streaked hands.

"Post," he grunted.

William rose and stretched out a hand. "Thank you, sir."

He saw the surprised look on his landlord's face before he remembered that dukes rarely thanked anyone for something as simple as bringing up the post. Nor did they call a mere commoner, sir. But before he could say anything more, the door was closed.

"A letter each," William said quietly, thrusting John's into his hands.

"Thank you," his brother muttered. "As I was saying…"

John continued speaking, but William barely heard him. His eyes had fallen onto the letter addressed to him and the seal which had closed it. A. Axwick?

His fingers fumbled as he opened it and pulled out what appeared to be a formal invitation. His eyes drank in the words.

Your Grace, the Duke of Mercia, and his lordship, the Marquess of Gloucester;

Your presence is requested for tea with Lady Charlotte St. Maur at Number Fourteen, Queen Square, today at eleven o'clock.

It was one of the shortest invitations he had ever read, but it was clear enough. Charlotte had invited him and John, of course, to drink tea with her.

John's voice continued, but William could not concentrate. What did this invitation mean? If she wanted to spend more time with him, why had she invited John? Was the invitation a mere formality? He was still learning so much about the ways of nobility, and at every turn, he was about to make a misstep.

"You're not listening to me, are you?"

"What?" William looked up from his invitation and saw the disappointment in his brother's face. "Here."

He handed the invitation over and watched John's eyebrows rise as he read the short missive.

"Well, well!" laughed John. "And will you go?"

"I am not the only one invited," pointed out William. "I do not believe one of us can attend without the other."

"I am more than happy to attend. Lady Charlotte is an excellent conversationalist, and I have naught to do until luncheon as it is," John said, reaching out for a large, burnt potato.

"What do you think she means by it?" William had not intended to speak aloud, but it was impossible to keep the question to himself.

John's eyebrows raised. "By an invitation? I would say she would like us to have tea with her. What more could she mean?"

Tea it was to be then, and he could no easier fathom what Charlotte's thoughts were than his own. What did he want from her, from this invitation for this morning? He wanted her body, certainly. Their moment outside the Pump Room had certainly proven that.

He wanted more. He wanted to know her thoughts, her opinions. Why did she rarely speak? Was she afraid that he would not take her seriously—or perhaps, that he would?

So lost was he in his thoughts, that it felt like no time had passed when he found himself knocking on the door of her home.

"I hope she has cake," John said, stamping his feet in the brisk morning. "I am famished."

William could barely think. It seemed an age before the door was opened, and there stood Matthews. The butler looked somehow much taller and more imposing than when they had last visited.

"Your Grace, your lordship," said Matthews quietly with a frown that made William's nerves increase. "You are expected."

He may as well have said *you are to be executed*, for that was the feeling it imparted. John, however, appeared to be immune to Matthews's displeasure.

John stepped forward without a care, and William followed.

There was a door open to his left, and John strode in. William hesitated. This was her territory, their first meeting on her own soil. Through the doorway came the welcoming tones of a woman and

John's laughter.

This is no time to wait around, William told himself. *Move, man!*

Somehow, he managed to walk into the room. Charlotte wore a simple day dress more suited for a miss rather than a lady. There was a nervous smile on her face as she indicated he should be seated.

William's heart softened. After all his wonderings and concern, there was no ulterior motive here, just a desire, it seemed, to spend more time together.

"I never thought I would find myself the chaperone," John joked as the three of them sat down. "Fear not, my lady, I will guard you against my brother if needed!"

It was well-meant but badly done. William saw the faint flush on Charlotte's cheeks as she took in his brother's words, but John seemed utterly oblivious.

"Well, I cannot tell you how pleased we were to receive your invitation, Lady Charlotte. This will be the best food and drink we have had all day!"

"Indeed? You have not found your lodgings to your liking?"

"Not at all," John said with a sigh. "Will was saying only this morning that we should look for another situation. Were you not, Will?"

William opened his mouth but found no words forthcoming. Charlotte looked up, tea in hand, and passed it over to him silently. He accepted it.

"Yes," said John calmly, a little frown at his brother's silence but more than able to continue the conversation. "We had not expected to be in Bath so long, and so the rooms we acquired for our duration do not suit."

William took a long sip of tea as John continued speaking. What was happening to him? He was not usually struck dumb in any setting, but it was not difficult to see why this would finally defeat him.

His eyes took in the plush leather wallpaper, the delicate embroidery on every surface, the rich, gilt frames around paintings of women who looked remarkably like Charlotte all around the room.

This was the parlor of a lady, a truly noble one.

This was not his setting. No, this sort of formal place was more suited to a man of rank and breeding. Even when a major, invited to some of the best homes where they were billeted, William had never felt comfortable.

John had fallen silent, and William glanced at Charlotte and saw her blush again.

"It is very cold for the time of year," he managed before sipping his tea again. The weather. He was talking about the weather?

"Yes," Charlotte said quietly. "And yet, I think it will be warmer soon. The cold cannot last."

Silence fell again, save for the ticking of a grandfather clock. William looked at John for help but saw his brother was grinning. This was entertainment for him, though torture for William.

After another ten minutes of awkward conversation, William was almost at a breaking point. Should he just leave? Was there any point in staying if Charlotte was to be so quiet?

John sneezed. As he closed his eyes to blow his nose, Charlotte grinned at William and winked.

William smiled back at her, relief pouring into his heart. Of course, why had he not seen it immediately? It was John's presence that was preventing her from speaking openly. But surely there was a way…

"Tell me, Lady Charlotte," he said suddenly. "Did you enjoy our walk back from the Pump Room?"

Their eyes met, and he saw she perfectly understood him.

"I did, even though we did not find Bert."

William grinned but was prevented from responding by his brother, who said, "Who is Bert?"

Charlotte laughed, and William's heart leapt as she replied, "It is of no matter."

"Bert is not a common name," John persisted, helping himself to another biscuit. "I knew a Bert before. He was in your regiment, wasn't he, William? A good man. Where is he now?"

William looked down at his hands and felt a shadow pass over him. "He did not return. He is buried somewhere in France, I think."

Sorrow flittered across Charlotte's face.

"This is not the appropriate conversation for a lady," William said hastily. "We should speak about different things."

"I would like to hear more about it." She poured herself another cup of tea, perhaps to avoid William's eyes as she spoke. "More about your time in the army, Your Grace. If you do not mind. What was it like?"

William scrabbled to find the words to describe some of the best and worst times of his life. "I…"

John laughed. "Now, you will not hear a true account from my brother, Lady Charlotte. Better to ask me, one of the true soldiers!"

"True soldiers?" Charlotte repeated. "I do not understand."

"It is quite simple, my lady," John said. "My brother was a major. He had all the best food, beds, and places to sleep."

"You do not have a clue what you are talking about," snapped William. "You never went into battle, John. Never even saw the enemy! Once you have seen what I have seen, you would not jest about it. You would not claim to be a true soldier. True soldiers were men like Bert, and he was not the only one who did not come home."

Silence fell once again, but this was not quiet full of anticipation for the next part of the conversation. This was painful.

Damn and blast it. Why had he brought all this up? What was wrong with him? Why would he say things that upset Charlotte and embarrassed John?

William stared into his cup of tea, and when he finally lifted his head, his brother was abashed.

Charlotte had not looked away. "It must feel strange coming back to England after seeing such things."

He nodded, unable to find the words to respond.

"Almost as though you cannot return to the England you knew," she continued softly. "That England is gone, and a strange one left in its place."

William's mouth fell open. How could she possibly know? "You are not about to tell us that you, too, have seen a battlefield, are you?"

Charlotte laughed and shook her head. "No, but I have lived through serious changes. There is no returning to your old life. No matter how much one may wish it."

"I have never heard anyone explain it that way before," William said quietly, "nor that well."

No further words were needed. They understood each other.

"I have much to learn," John said quietly.

William drained his teacup and placed it back onto its saucer. "And I am glad my younger brother never had to," he said. "No man should. Now the war is over, I hope it will be many generations before anyone else has to."

"I believe that to be unlikely," Charlotte said quietly.

How was it that she understood not only his words but the meaning beneath them? He had never encountered a person, let alone a woman, who was able to pierce through his mutterings and see the truth.

"Indeed," he said heavily. "If the posturing of nations does not stop soon…"

His voice trailed off, and they all fell into silence.

Was this what polite society discussed? William had no idea, having spent so little time in it. This felt more intimate, more honest than any other conversation he had had since entering Bath. And it was Charlotte; she had drawn it from him.

"Who would be a politician, eh?" John said with a shake of his head. "I was just thinking the other day, Lady Charlotte…"

What was William doing here? For all the trappings of family name, title, and wealth, he was just a soldier. It was all he had known for so long, how to fight, how to protect, how to give, and take orders.

Charlotte was a lady. A lady born and bred. She needed, nay, deserved someone who had grown up knowing which fork to use for the fish course.

The chiming of the grandfather clock interrupted his thoughts.

"Is that the time?" John stood hastily. "I do apologize, Lady Charlotte, but I am needed elsewhere. I had no idea how much time had flown!"

Charlotte rose to her feet, and William almost staggered to his own, as she said, "Please, do not worry yourself, my lord. I have an appointment in town also."

"Perhaps I can escort you," William offered.

She smiled. "I would enjoy that." She rang the bell and moved back to her seat.

As she did so, John whispered to his brother, "You could have picked a more joyful topic for wooing."

"What did you expect from me?" William shrugged with a murmur.

John shook his head as a footman entered the room with Charlotte's pelisse.

"Well, I am this way," John said with a wink as the three of them headed for the door and stepped outside. "And I am sure you are both that way. Thank you, Lady Charlotte, for a delightful morning."

He bowed and started off down the street, whistling as he went.

William grinned at Charlotte. "I thought we'd never lose him."

"He is like an excitable puppy."

"Yes, and a badly trained one!"

"He is good company," she countered as they fell in step with each other. "I like him."

"I cannot disagree with you. Some gentlemen are unfortunate in their brothers, whereas I have never found his companionship irksome."

"I experienced both, I believe," Charlotte said softly. "My brother, Richard, is a true gentleman, and yet Arnold, who came from the same stock and same home, was utterly different. Cold. Cruel, even."

They turned a corner, and both simultaneously took a step to the left to avoid some horse droppings.

"I am doubly fortunate," William said, breathing out heavily. "I have never had any complaints when spending time with my siblings."

"And why do you wish to spend time with me?"

The question had come from nowhere, but it was certainly Charlotte who had spoken. Her eyes blazed as she looked at him, just a hint of embarrassment tinging her cheeks.

"Spend time with you?" he asked, stalling for time. "What do you mean?"

She had stopped now, and he mirrored her, allowing the flow of people to continue around them.

"I mean…does the line of Mercia not need an heir? I first made your acquaintance when chaperoning you for a potential wife. Do you…do you not still need to seek one?"

It was the most vulnerable and direct statement she had ever spoken, and William swallowed before formulating his response.

"I have John," he said carefully, his gaze focused on her face. "He will have to do as an heir, for now."

"I am in earnest, William. No other gentleman is seeking out my company, and I need to know why."

He opened his mouth to say something clever but immediately closed it again. Why was he so drawn to Charlotte? No other lady had driven him this wild physically, that was certain. Her maturity and beauty combined were enough to keep him up at night.

But it was more than that. Her conversation was so much more riveting than any other. She had sincere concerns and deep thoughts, solid opinions, and was not afraid to share them. And the way she laughed—it was unlike anyone he knew.

"Because I enjoy myself the most when I am with you," he said simply.

Charlotte's gaze dropped to her hands, her fingers twisting. "You are fortunate that I am not younger, Your Grace, or I would consider that a flirtation."

"You should," he said seriously, reaching out to take her moving fingers in his. "More than flirtation. Charlotte…"

A noise ahead stopped his words. Shouts and shrieks, some in laughter and some in pain.

William's gaze searched out the cause of the disturbance and saw where it was coming from a little further down the road. His blood started to boil.

An elderly gentleman in a military uniform, from what William could see, was seated on the ground. His arms were over his head to protect himself from the stones being pelted at him by three youths who were all laughing.

"Oh, no!" Charlotte exclaimed beside him.

William had to do something.

"Hey!" He ran toward them as fast as he could, anger building inside him. "How dare you!"

The three offenders cared little for what William had to say and stared at him, waiting for whatever came next.

"Who are you to stop us?" the tallest one challenged.

William's attention went to the gentleman on the ground, his hands still covering his face.

Poor sod.

"You cannot tell us what to do!" another of the lads called out.

All three were dressed in apprentice garb, feeling joy in the harm they were inflicting on the old man. Not gentlemen, not even craftsmen yet. Just three boys with naught to do but harm another fellow human being.

William straightened to his full height. For a moment, he was back in the army, a major shouting at privates who had been caught in the act of wrongdoing.

But he had no jurisdiction here, no authority. The law had been broken, certainly, but what could he do, drag them to prison?

Justice must be done. He was a duke, which held weight in society no matter where he was. No one else had stepped forward, although several people were walking past, their eyes averted.

Perhaps the rage showed on his face, for the moment he took a step forward, the boys shrank back, appearing afraid.

"I wasn't doing no harm," one of them said.

Charlotte had reached his side as he spoke, "No harm? What in God's name possessed you to start throwing stones at this man? Has he not sacrificed enough, fighting for his country? Wasn't it enough of a disgrace that he was forced to live on the streets? You should be honoring him and feeding him, rather than throwing stones!"

They looked at each other, shame clear on their faces. Charlotte had not said a word, and he could not tell whether she was disgusted by the way he was treating these boys or shocked at his angry tone.

"Come on," one of them said, and the three of them slipped away into the crowd that had gathered around them.

"T-thank you, sir."

Kneeling before the elderly man, William looked into his eyes. Without saying a word, he pulled out his pocketbook and offered the stranger a five-pound note.

"For you," he said gruffly.

The man shook his head in refusal. "Five pounds? God knows I need it, sir, but I cannot take it."

William had already dropped the note into the gentleman's lap, stood tall, and started walking away. He had to walk, had to move. He had to do something to forget his anger.

Charlotte slipped her hand into his. "That was a very brave thing you just did."

William felt a little guilty for the spark of pleasure her words brought. "The idea of our men coming back here to live in poverty, suffering to no end, displeases me more than I can express."

"It is a disgrace," she said softly.

He nodded. "Who knows that I would have been any different?"

As they walked, Charlotte looked back at the man still seated on the pavement. "You would never have lived like that."

William stopped in his tracks. "Why not? I came home to a title, but others return to no family, no friends, and no livelihood. They bring back the demons of the battlefield with them."

He had not intended his voice to be so loud nor his grip on her hand to be so tight. Charlotte swallowed, and he released her hand, lowering his gaze to the ground.

"There is so much I do not understand," she said, "but I am willing to learn."

All the bitterness disappeared from his heart. She never failed to surprise him. How many other ladies would have even thought it, let alone said the words?

It was a few more minutes before he said quietly, "I should not have allowed my temper to get the better of me, especially with you."

"I understand."

"Would you say yes if I proposed, Charlotte? In seriousness?" He stopped again, watching her intently.

Her eyes flickered to her left. "This is where my appointment is."

William turned to look. They were outside a dressmaker, and Charlotte was avoiding his gaze.

"You have not answered my question."

"Is it possible for you to go ten minutes without proposing to me?" She smiled at him gently. "William, I do not believe you could make me that offer in seriousness. Good day, Your Grace."

CHAPTER NINE

I T WAS THE noise of the hooves on the cobbles and the neighing of the horses that caught her attention. Charlotte smiled as she looked up through the window to see a carriage pull up in Queen Square with the Axwick livery painted carefully on the side of the door.

They were home.

Looking down at the letter still in her lap, she reread her brother's handwriting.

We will leave early to avoid any nonsense on the road and will aim to be with you by ten o'clock at the latest.

She glanced at the clock on the mantelpiece. It had just chimed a quarter past twelve. Well, they had their excuses now, of course. The Duke and Duchess of Axwick could be as late as they wanted in their condition.

Folding up the letter and placing it on the small table beside her, Charlotte called out, "Matthews, they are here!"

There was no answering shout from the butler, and a frown of confusion creased her brow until the sound of the front door opening echoed. He had already seen them, and as Charlotte peered through the window, she saw the elderly butler open the door to the carriage and offer a hand.

She watched as Tabitha stepped down, straightening her pelisse as she stood and waited for her husband to dismount from the carriage on the other side. It was still too early for anyone who did not know Tabitha to see that she was with child, but if you knew what you were looking for, it was clear as day. The gentle curve of her stomach, the way she cupped it with her hand. Protective. Nurturing.

Charlotte rose and smoothed down her own gown. She had been looking forward to their visit for days, and this was no time to start becoming envious. This was excellent news for her brother and sister-in-law. *You will not tie yourself in knots about this,* she warned herself silently.

A few steps brought her into the hallway where the couple stood.

"I wish you would be more careful, Tabitha," Richard was saying sternly as his wife threw herself into Charlotte's arms. "Now, really!"

Charlotte laughed at the suddenness of it all, and the sisterly affection she was showered with by a woman who, really, she barely knew. Her courtship with her brother had been so short, there was barely time to become acquainted before they traipsed up the aisle.

"I am careful," shot back Tabitha as Matthews helped her out of her pelisse. "Do not concern yourself, Richard, you will give yourself gout."

"Gout! You are the one who is in a delicate state, not I!"

Tabitha rolled her eyes and winked at Charlotte as she removed her bonnet. "Nonsense."

Charlotte glanced at her brother, who looked apoplectic. "Please, Tabitha, go and sit down in the drawing room."

"Sit down? I have been sitting down in a carriage for this very age! The last thing I wish to do is sit down." Tabitha smiled at Charlotte and continued, "Now Charlotte, you must tell me—wait a moment…"

Charlotte and Richard waited as Tabitha's voice trailed away, her cheeks went pale, and she put a hand to her mouth.

"You must excuse me. Matthews, I need a bowl!"

She rushed down the corridor toward the kitchen in a whirl of skirts, and the door slammed behind her.

"Should we go after her?" Charlotte asked anxiously. "Is she quite well?"

"No," said Richard heavily. "But that does not stop her from attempting to act like she is." He saw his sister's worried face and smiled. "You know Tabitha is with child. According to Doctor Lawrence, this is a completely natural stage of the process, but if you ask me, it feels like hard work. I do not know why any woman bothers to put up with it!"

She returned his smile. "I think once the baby has arrived, you may think a little differently. Tabitha certainly will."

"We were delayed two hours because of all this stopping and vomiting out of carriages. I shall be glad to see the end of it."

Their conversation was interrupted by a figure coming down the stairs.

"Ah, Danvers," Charlotte said.

Her lady's maid stopped at the foot of the stairs and bobbed a curtsey.

"Would you mind seeing to the Duchess of Axwick?" Charlotte said quietly. "She is in the kitchen in search of a bowl and requires assistance?"

Danvers blinked. "A bowl, my lady?"

Richard smiled. "My wife expects to be confined by the end of the summer."

Understanding was swift. "I shall go and look after Her Grace this moment," said Danvers with a nod.

"And in the meantime, let's sit down," Richard said, not bothering to wait for Charlotte's reply before turning to step into the drawing room.

They seated themselves on either side of the fireplace, the fire blazing. Charlotte's mind was with Tabitha in the kitchen. What was it like to know there was a child growing inside you? How did it feel to have one's body utterly taken over to the needs of a baby you had not even met yet?

"I do not believe I have given my congratulations in person," she said hastily, aware that her role as hostess was being neglected. Really, it was strange to play host to one's brother in the place where you had once lived together.

"You have not," her brother replied with a grin. "Do not worry about it, we have been inundated with congratulations from all. And really, until the child arrives, I am attempting not to get too excited."

"You are not?"

Richard shook his head. "The doctor recommended not to. So many things can happen between now and when the babe is due to enter this world. He…he says we should not expect an easy time of it."

Charlotte could hear the concern in his voice, both for his child and his wife, but did not pursue it. Her brother was a quiet soul. When he was ready to share more, he would.

"I am pleased to see both of you—or all three of you," she corrected with a laugh. "But I must say, Richard, I am not entirely sure whether it was wise for you to travel all this way, just for two days here in Bath. Why come so far to stay so little?"

He shrugged. "We wanted to see you but have no other desire to remain in Bath. Besides, the air here is too thick for a woman with child. I would rather have her back in the safety of Stonehaven Lacey."

There was something so different about him that Charlotte was quite startled. This was not the brother she knew, the one she had known for the last thirty years. He was younger, somehow. More carefree, less concerned about the world. The heaviness of their family's debts had gone, which must form part of it, but there was something more.

"You examine me."

She jumped and saw her brother smiling.

"Only to understand you better," she said hastily. "It is remarkable, the change in you. Marriage clearly agrees with you!"

"I will admit, and only to you, Charlotte, for I know you are the soul of discretion, that marriage is more than I could ever have wished for."

It was strange, hearing those words from him. He had been so adamant for years that he would never wed, that the St. Maur branch of the Axwick line would end. Balls, dances, card parties, even polite visiting, he had avoided them all. He had been determined to keep to his own vow.

And that had all changed when he had met Miss Tabitha Chesworth. Or more accurately, Charlotte reminded herself, when she had introduced them.

"I was a fool to attempt to avoid it," he was saying. "With each passing day, I realize the extent of my idiocy. If you ask me, Lotty, everyone should marry!"

Her stomach twisted, and her gaze fell to her hands in her lap.

"Oh, damn, Charlotte. Forgive me."

She looked up to see Richard's face, complete embarrassment.

"I spoke in haste and without thought. Please forgive me."

Charlotte smiled and reached out to squeeze his hand. "You worry over nothing, Axwick. I am not offended, nor do I believe I should be. You wish to celebrate the happiness you have found; it is only natural."

The door suddenly opened, and two women walked in.

"Peppermint, I say again," Danvers said as she led Tabitha into the room. "Just a little on your pillow, the herb or oil, and it will work wonders."

"I shall have to tell my lady's maid," Tabitha said with a weak smile as she allowed herself to be deposited on a chaise longue. "You must think me very silly, Charlotte. I do apologize."

"I've never known a couple to apologize so often! You are with child, Tabitha, and I do not believe anyone in that circumstance is required to apologize at all."

"Thank goodness," Tabitha said faintly.

Danvers exchanged a look with Charlotte. Her maid evidently knew what she was doing.

"Thank you, Danvers, that will be all," Charlotte said quietly.

As the door shut behind the servant, Richard rolled his eyes. "It is fortunate we are with family and not guests!"

His wife laughed without opening her eyes. "It is good that you are too far away from me to reach you, or I would hit you!"

Charlotte's gaze flickered between them, concern sweeping across her heart. Were they angry, ill-suited for one another?

It was only then that she saw their laughter and realized they had only been jesting. There was much to marriage she simply did not understand and never would. Unless, of course, William Lennox was in any way serious about anything he had said to her. He was so difficult to understand. She knew so little of him, and there was no way to discover more about him unless...

"There are many new people in Bath this Season, and I have been making the acquaintance of some of them."

Richard leaned back in his chair. "Really? I did not think there was anyone else worth knowing with whom the family was not acquainted. Anyone of particular interest?"

Charlotte swallowed. Her brother was an intelligent man. How direct could she be without him guessing the reason for bringing up such a topic? She did not want to reveal how she felt about William.

"Do you mean Miss Darby, the lady you encountered at our wedding?" Tabitha asked.

"Miss Darby?" Richard snorted. "I would not consider her a suitable acquaintance for you, Charlotte. Are you not bored to tears by her?"

"I would not say Miss Darby has become an intimate acquaintance," Charlotte said slowly. "I accompanied her to the opera and on a separate occasion, a carriage ride with some gentlemen. It is actually the two gentlemen that I have become more acquainted with. One…one in particular."

Tabitha sat up hastily, the blanket falling to the carpet. "Are you telling me you are being courted?"

"Of course not," Richard said easily. When Charlotte did not respond, he leaned forward and repeated, "Of course not, that is not what you are saying at all. Is it, Lotty?"

Was it possible to keep calm in such an unexpected situation? "I said nothing of the sort."

"But that is what is happening, is it not?" Tabitha asked eagerly.

She paused before responding. In truth, she was not entirely sure what she was to William. Her own emotions, at least, were more clear. She felt more strongly about him than anyone else and would not have permitted him to kiss her in the alleyway if she had not.

Perhaps it would not be prudent to reveal that *particular* detail to her overprotective brother.

"I enjoy both of the Lennox brothers' company. Have either of you been introduced to William or John Lennox?"

Apparently appeased by her calmness, her brother leaned back in his seat. "I once met the previous Duke of Mercia, a very elderly gentleman who rarely ventured into society. Arnold wished to make his acquaintance, so we both went, but it was a short and uninteresting visit. I saw no evidence of a wife, I must say, and was not aware he had a son."

Charlotte made a personal note to find out more about this surprising inheritance line. Without really being aware that she was speaking aloud, she muttered, "Then I wonder how William–I mean, the current duke, received the title. Uncle? Cousin?"

It appeared that Tabitha was finally losing interest in the conversation. "As so many of them do, I suppose. Through a junior branch of the line."

"Have you met William or John, Tabitha?" Charlotte asked.

Her sister-in-law frowned in concentration. "I remember there was some sort of scandal a few years ago—so I must have."

Charlotte stiffened. It had not been her intention to stir up gossip about Honora, the sister who had so tragically disappeared from the lives of her brothers. William had been so clearly distraught at even the thought of her somewhere out there in the world.

"Scandal?" Richard said. "I do not like the sound of that. I am not entirely convinced you should be mixing with scandalous dukes, Charlotte."

She sighed wryly. "I know the tale, Richard, and it is a sad one, not a scandalous one. I do not believe I would wish it on any family."

"I cannot remember the exact details," mused Tabitha, "but I can tell you that Major Lennox was an absolute rake."

Charlotte's heart turned cold in an instant. "A-a rake?"

Her sister-in-law nodded. "Oh, yes, a notorious womanizer. He had a favorite in every town and village in France when his regiment was over there, and tales quickly found their way back to England whenever they wintered here. Goodness, the stories my mother attempted to tell me, you would think they were a plot by Byron rather than reality!"

It was not possible, and yet Tabitha had no reason to lie. Charlotte attempted to keep her breathing slow and steady. She had asked the question because she wanted to know what kind of a man William was. She had to be brave enough to face the answer.

"And many of them wept when he left the country for good," Tabitha was saying, oblivious to how her words were upsetting Charlotte. "He was their protector, of course, and by all accounts, a fine lover."

"Tabitha!" Richard looked absolutely appalled.

"I am only repeating the gossip!" she said defensively, opening her eyes to look at her husband. "And Charlotte did ask, after all."

"Yes, well, that is of no importance," he said hastily, glancing at

Charlotte. "We all have family members that we disapprove of and would not agree with, just look at Arnold, our brother. Damned fool if ever there was one. I am sure this duke that Charlotte has met does not mix with this Major Lennox."

Charlotte swallowed. There was nothing for it. She would have to speak, and though it would shock her brother, it certainly hurt her far more.

"Actually, Richard," she said quietly, "Major Lennox came to the title of Duke of Mercia a few years ago. They are one and the same man."

There was a moment of silence.

"Ah," was all her brother managed.

Charlotte had no idea where to look. She could not meet her brother's eye, nor his wife's, and yet there was nowhere else in the room she could gaze. Pain radiated from her heart, and the discomfort was so thick in the air, she could have cut it with a knife.

William the womanizer. William the rake. William, the favorite of women from France.

William, who had courted countless ladies before her, who knew exactly what a lady wanted to hear, knew how to tease her, and convince her to...to what?

How could she trust a man with such a reputation? How could she be sure that he meant anything that he ever said to her?

"You know, I feel ready to eat something now," Tabitha announced, sitting up.

Her husband laughed. "I am not surprised, even when you are in the depths of illness, you always find it within yourself to eat something!"

He rose and rang the bell by the fireplace, giving Charlotte a moment to collect herself. She would not betray her true feelings, not now. She needed to think on this alone, and it would be many hours before she was afforded that luxury.

"Luncheon, Matthews," Richard said grandly as the butler entered the room. "On trays in here, if you would not mind, my wife is still feeling a little delicate."

"At once, Your Grace," Matthews bowed. As if he had been expecting the summons at any moment, a stream of footmen appeared behind him, bringing in lunch.

Charlotte raised an eyebrow at her butler, who gave a brief smile.

"Danvers came to see me before she returned to her linens, my lady, and advised that her grace would likely feel more comfortable eating lunch in the drawing room."

Tabitha looked astonished, but Richard laughed. "I should have known! You have a good one there, Charlotte, I would not let her go in a hurry!"

Charlotte demurred as a silver tray covered in delicious food was placed beside her. Despite the effort her cook had evidently put in while the Duke and Duchess of Axwick were visiting, she could find no pleasure in eating.

While Tabitha and Richard managed to keep the conversation flowing with little pause, Charlotte saw her brother give her a concerned look at her, but he said nothing.

What was there to say? she thought bitterly. He had done nothing wrong. It was William who had lost her trust this afternoon.

CHAPTER TEN

"GOD'S TEETH, MAN, don't be stupid!"

John raised his eyebrows and shrugged. "I will say it again, Mercia, you seem tense this evening, ever since we left our rooms. Are you certain nothing is amiss?"

William growled rather than respond, his temper on edge but aware that in public, there was no more he could say.

His brother looked away to speak to the gentleman seated beside him, and William tried to breathe out slowly as the musicians at the recital started to tune their instruments.

This was madness. Snapping at his brother was not going to solve anything, and drawing attention to himself would make matters more complicated. If only he could return to the peaceful man he had always been.

John's foot bumped into his own.

"Keep to your side!" William said.

The people seated around them grew silent as all eyes shifted over to them seated in the front row of the Assembly Rooms, pride of place thanks to Lady Romeril's invitation.

John turned away from his brother and repositioned his feet in an exaggerated way. William's cheeks heated.

"What," murmured his brother in a low voice, "has got you in such a terrible temper, William?"

William sighed. It was not his brother's doing, and he shamed himself by taking it out on him. "I apologize, John. I am bad-tempered tonight. There is no excuse."

John gripped his shoulder, then turned to continue his conversation.

That was the thing about brothers—one did not always have to explain things.

Not that he was entirely sure that he could explain it. It didn't make sense, these letters from Charlotte.

Unable to prevent himself, William reached into his pocket and pulled out the pages Charlotte had sent him in response to invitations to dine, for walks, to a card party, and to this musical recital. He had only started sending more formal invitations when her name had not appeared in the Pump Rooms book for a week, and there had been no response from knocking on her door, other than Matthews's stern frown.

> *Your Grace,*
>
> *I must send you my sincere apologies that I am unable to attend the Coulsons' card party with you tomorrow evening. I am sure you will have an enjoyable evening.*
>
> *Lady Charlotte St. Maur*

William's jaw clenched. What did it mean? Why was she avoiding him so concertedly? And here was another one.

> *Your Grace,*
>
> *I have no interest in a walk at the present time. Please share your invitation with another lady who is.*
>
> *Lady Charlotte St. Maur*

No interest? He could not fault her letters for politeness, but they were so distant. The sort of letters one would send to an elderly aunt whom you did not wish to visit. After all they had discussed, shared with each other, why did she suddenly have no desire to see him?

He sighed heavily as he read the letter he had received most recently.

Your Grace,

I regret to inform you that I am no longer available for engagements of any kind. Please cease contacting me on this matter, for my interest in such things will not change.

Lady Charlotte St. Maur

Cease contacting her as though he could wipe her from his mind? What had happened?

William's gaze wandered lazily around the room. He watched the musicians without much interest—even studied some of the people, but all he could think about was Charlotte.

He loved her. There was no denying it, no reason to, except he had never had to work so hard for a woman's affection. There were instances when he was sure she felt the same.

But not enough.

The violinist nudged the viola player beside him, and they both frowned at William. He shifted uncomfortably in the wooden seat and allowed his gaze to drift to the candles on the wall.

Why not? What was holding her back?

It was in these moments that he wished, more than anything, that Honora was still with them. John was intelligent, but Honora had a softness of heart and an understanding soul. She could have explained to him why Charlotte had placed herself at odds with him. Perhaps she could have even spoken with Charlotte, helped her to understand that he was in earnest.

William sighed. Wherever Honora was, he wanted her back. Thinking on it would bring him naught but pain. Though he hoped to see her at every event he attended. And now there was Charlotte.

It was strange. When he had been a soldier, marriage had been absolutely out of the question. Who wanted a war-worn soldier for a husband? A few ladies had accepted him into their beds, but he had gained more of a reputation for wooing than for bedding.

Now that he had a title and had found the right woman, she was not interested.

Someone nudged him hard on the shoulder, and William turned around with a snarl to see John. "What?"

John pointed toward the entrance. Irritated beyond belief to have had his thoughts disturbed once more, William turned to see Charlotte enter the room. Not alone, though. As his mind whirled, he saw two people with her—a young lady with too much rouge on her cheeks to be respectable, and a gangly gentleman who looked as though he didn't know how to walk properly.

William sighed. Once again, Charlotte was acting as a chaperone. It would explain the drab blue gown several years out of fashion, the lack of jewels, and the complete lack of care spent on her hair. Not forgetting the look of boredom on her face.

Despite all that, her beauty eclipsed the others around her, despite their finery.

How could no one else see her remarkable beauty? It drove him mad the world did not notice.

"Lady Charlotte!" he shouted without thinking.

The crowd gathered to hear Mozart stared, but William did not care. His spirits had risen as soon as she had shown up. Another chance to spend an evening with her.

"There are seats here," he called out. "Lady Charlotte!"

There were frowns around the room and a few murmurs from mothers to daughters, but William paid them no heed. What care he that Mamas considered him a loose cannon? His brother John knew enough pretty young ladies for both of them, and the dukedom seemed far more important to most mothers than his ineptitude in public.

She turned and saw him, her gray eyes meeting his. She smiled, but there was no warmth. Then she looked away and sat with the couple on the other side of the aisle.

Just as William made up his mind to force Charlotte to speak with him, there was another nudge to his shoulder.

"Miss Howarth, I do not believe my brother has had the pleasure of making your acquaintance yet?"

"My lord, I mean, Your Grace," she spluttered, cheeks red. "Your brother was telling me how interested you are in…"

"How do you do." William nodded distractedly despite the beauty of the girl before him.

"I was saying to Miss Seton the other day it would be such an honor to meet the new Duke of Mercia."

"Yes," he said. "Please do excuse me, Miss Howarth, John, but I need to go and speak to…"

"And here *is* Miss Seton, good evening!" John's voice overrode his as another lady came toward them.

William groaned. This was intolerable, and now that Miss Seton had joined them, he could no longer see Charlotte. Craning his neck awkwardly around her and a gentleman with a hat far too tall, he caught a glimpse of her.

Charlotte's mouth was set in a hard line. William knew that face. Someone had said something impertinent. What a shame she was so graceful. Someone with less breeding would be rude in turn, but not her. She was incapable of being inconsiderate even when provoked.

"I do like your gown," one of the girls John had rounded up was saying to the other. "I think it so brave to wear something that old fashioned here in Bath."

William was paying attention enough to see the spark of fury on Miss Seton's face as she responded. "It is funny you should say that, Lady Romeril was just complimenting me on my return to classic style. But then, you are probably not aware, my *dear* Miss Howarth, all the salons in London are graced with this style."

William gritted his teeth. He was not going to stand here and listen to women talk about gowns.

"You must excuse me," he said. "I need to speak with…"

"Ah, here is Miss Ashbrooke!" John said.

William did not see how his brother managed it, so many women attracted to their corner of the room.

"Mercia, have you met…"

"Enough." William laid a hand on John's arm. "Enough, do you understand?"

He grinned. "I have no idea what you are talking about. Is there such a thing as enough?"

"When was the last time you spoke with Miss Darby?"

William had not intended his words to be harsh, but his brother flinched as though he had branded him with a hot poker. His shoulders slumped. "Over two weeks. She has not responded to either of my notes, and I heard she was being courted by Marnmouth."

The ladies around them chattered on as William tightened his grip on his brother's arm. Now here, finally, was an explanation for that bad temper a week ago. "If she is truly meant for you, and you for her, you need to fight for her, Gloucester. Or someone else will win her."

John glanced at Charlotte. "About to practice what you preach?"

William nodded wearily. "Something like that. I will tell you more in our rooms, after the concert."

Without waiting for a response, he pushed his way past the giggling girls as the conductor rose to the podium to a round of applause. The audience took their seats.

"Excuse me, sir," whispered a haughty looking woman. "But you are in my way."

William inclined his head in silent apology but kept his eyes on Charlotte. There was an empty seat in the row in front of her. He hoped no one would beat him to it.

"Why," he said quietly, dropping into the seat as the musicians began, "did you not come over and sit with me? John would have been pleased to see you."

He had to twist in his seat to look at her, but Charlotte did not meet his gaze. "I am here with Miss Catherine Morse and Mr. Timothy Barnes. Are you acquainted with Mr. Barnes or Miss Morse?"

"No, I am not, nor have any wish to be," he snapped. "And all three of you could have joined us, if you had wanted."

Her eyes still did not rise to meet his. "You had more than enough company."

William glanced over at John, who was seated with three ladies, all staring at William. In fact, the majority of the room appeared to be staring at him. He grimaced as he contemplated the gossip which would undoubtedly emerge from tonight's behavior: an upstart duke who has no comprehension of civility, no doubt.

He groaned. "Charlotte, you know me better than that. You know I have no interest in ladies parading before me. You are the only one I asked to dance."

"Shush!"

The remonstrance was loud and furious, and William looked around to see the conductor himself glaring. Bowing his head in a silent apology, William gestured that the conductor should continue. The short man sniffed and tapped his baton on the music stand.

He would get a reputation for himself, if he was not careful. It would not do to ostracize himself entirely from good society, even if he couldn't help but act impulsively whenever around Charlotte.

William waited for a few bars of music, then twisted in his seat to speak with her again. She was smiling—though it disappeared once she realized she had been spotted.

Fire sparked in his stomach. It was all a game with Charlotte, a way for her to tease him, to tempt him but never offer him what he wanted.

Well, he knew what he wanted, and he had asked for it enough times. Now he was going to take it.

Ignoring the horrified gasps from the audience, William grabbed Charlotte's arm and rose to his feet, pulling her along the row toward the aisle.

"Your Grace!"

Her startled cry didn't slow him down, and neither did the startled whispers all around them. The notorious gossip, Mrs. Bryant, muttered to her neighbor, but William did not care.

The moment he had touched her arm, even through his white gloves, the whole evening had come alive. Colors had appeared again, the music rose around him, and it did not matter that Charlotte was staring as though he had gone mad as he pulled her down the aisle to the door.

The freezing night air hit his face, and he gasped at the shock of it.

"What do you think you are doing?" Charlotte wrenched her arm free. "There are two people in there completely unchaperoned!"

"To hell with them," William said. "Finally, we can talk in peace."

Her glare had not disappeared as they stood outside. "Although you may find this hard to believe, I was actually looking forward to that recital—and the only reason I was invited was to act as Miss Morse's chaperone."

He scoffed. God, it was good to be with her again. Why did every second not in Charlotte's company seem like time completely wasted?

"It was Mozart," she was saying, "my favorite composer, and one who is indelicately played by most musicians. I should go right back in there and enjoy it with Miss Morse!"

She moved toward the door and hesitated. William stood unmoving and silent.

"You...you are not going to stop me?" Her expression held suspicion.

"No. Charlotte, I think I have made myself quite plain. I like you.

Though I hesitate to admit it to you, I…I am falling in love with you." The words sounded strange spoken aloud, but William had to be brave. It was time to speak out. "I enjoy your company, your conversation. You have never been a chaperone to me, but a captivating lady. The question is, why do you insist on avoiding me?"

"I am very much the chaperone for the next generation. My time has gone. I will never marry now," she said, her eyes not meeting his as she added, "and I am not avoiding you."

That was enough for him. "You are doing it this very moment!" he exploded. "God's teeth, Charlotte, but you have sorely hurt me this past week."

Was that a flicker of regret, of concern? Whatever it was, it had disappeared from Charlotte's eyes as quickly as it had appeared.

"I do not see how," she said stiffly. "I merely was unable to meet with you for seven days. Surely your other…acquaintances have provided you with enough entertainment in the meantime?"

William stared at her. "Entertainment? If I had wished to be entertained, I would not be here in Bath, full of rigid rules and polite nothingness happening every day. Charlotte, I am still in Bath because of you! Every day this week, I wished to see you!"

Excitement pumped through his veins, and the desire to run, to punch someone, to kiss her, flooded through his mind all at once. What he wouldn't do to have this woman!

"I-I have heard differently." Her words were controlled, but her eyes were full of emotion, threatening to overspill. "I have learned more of you, Your Grace, since we last met, and I am sad to say, I did not like it."

All the energy that was flowing through William, disappeared in an instant. "Learned differently? Did not like what?"

Charlotte shook her head, clearly holding back tears. "And I am sorry to have joined the collection of ladies who fawn over you, sir. I should have known that you were not serious in your intentions toward me. Good evening, Your Grace."

Before William could say a word, before he could even think, she was walking away from him.

Collection?

"Charlotte, wait!" He rushed after her, moving ahead to prevent her from taking another step. "Do you not believe I should have the right to defend myself?"

She glared at him. "Why would I want to hear about all the ladies you have *bedded!*"

William stared at her. God's teeth, he should have known his reputation from the army would not have stayed there. Why had he not mentioned this to her before? Why had he not been as open and honest with her as he had been with any gentleman?

All this could have been prevented, and now he would have to suffer the consequences of his actions.

She was still glaring at him, but he could sense her desperation for a genuine answer. She wanted to be reassured. She wanted all of this to go away, but she also needed the truth.

"Charlotte," he said quietly, "before I met you, it is true, I courted other women. Did you think I had never spoken with another lady before?"

She swallowed, her gaze focused on his eyes. "No, that would be...I just do not understand, after having your choice, clearly, from the whole of France, why you are even considering me?"

There was the truth, the pain, the fear. She was confused about his sincerity. William sighed with relief.

"Charlotte, I find it strange you even have to ask."

"Well, I do," she said fiercely, taking a step away from him. "William, you have been described to me as a womanizer, a rake. How can I trust a man with such a reputation?"

He took a deep breath. "Dukes are supposed to have such a reputation, even if no one speaks of it. Would you tell me your brother never bedded a woman before he married?"

"How dare you say—"

"I meant," he said hastily, "that nobles are almost encouraged to sow their wild oats, and so are men in the army. It is only when we wish to return to civilized society and we meet a woman who…takes our breath away and could very well be the one we wish to spend our lives with, then is the moment we realize our pasts are not what we would wish."

She stared at him, evidently unconvinced. "So, you regret your past deeds?"

William did not hesitate. "Most of them. All of them, if they offend you. Charlotte, I have never hidden my opinions of you, my wishes for you, my desire for you. Is that not enough?"

Had he gone too far? Had he pushed her beyond her limits, restrained as she was to the duties of society, unaccustomed to rebelling in even the smallest way?

William watched as she hesitated, eyes flickering between him and the door. She was paralyzed with indecision, and it hurt him. Why could she not reach out to him, demonstrate once and for all that she cared for him, or did she not care enough?

"Forget I said anything, please," he said quietly, attempting to quell the pain in his voice. "I cannot turn back the clock and change what has occurred. So, if you wish to break our acquaintance, I will not contact you again. I hope you enjoy your recital, Lady Charlotte."

Turning away was the most difficult thing anyone could have asked of him, but William knew he had to do it. He could not chase this woman any longer, not without some sign of encouragement.

He had walked five steps before her hand found his.

"May I join you?"

William smiled, his heart singing. "It feels so absolutely perfect, having your hand in mine," he said gently as they walked leisurely down the dark street. "I have never experienced something so…so right in all my life."

Charlotte squeezed his fingers. "I…I think so, too."

"Then why do you not consider me a suitor?"

She did not pull away. After walking in silence, she said quietly, "William, I barely know you."

"You know me better than anyone," he said with a laugh. "Better than my own brother, I think at times. There I was, desperate to be close to you, and he was throwing those ladies at me, none of whom I wanted to speak with. You saw that the first time you met me, Charlotte, do not pretend you did not."

"And that first time was a few weeks ago!" Charlotte laughed, and he felt the tension in her hand. "William, I grew up with most of the nobility of England and Ireland, they are my cousins, neighbors, and friends. It was always assumed I would wed one of them."

"But you have not!"

"Listen to me."

William swallowed the numerous objections he wished to raise and nodded.

"For a lady of my family, you expect to know the person you marry for years before you eventually do. I do not mean an arranged marriage, although that is not unheard of. It is more…they are someone you know, your father knows, your mother knows. All his faults are a part of your own childhood. You know his family, too."

She lifted her gaze to his, and William could see they were bright with emotion. "You…you frighten me. Not because of who you are, but because I do not know how you became the person I see before me. A few weeks? A few weeks is not long enough to decide on buying a horse, let alone choosing a husband!"

He could hear the fear in her voice. William squeezed her hand and tried to pour out the feelings overwhelming him. "Sometimes a month is all you need," he said. "God, Charlotte, do you think I believed it would be this quick? I look at you and just know, I need you!"

"Well, I am not ready. You need to be patient."

William could not help but groan, pure frustration overwhelming him.

It was a mistake.

"Why are you so adamant I have to make a decision now?" Charlotte pulled her hand from his but continued to walk alongside him. "There is no rush."

"I am being honest."

She frowned as they passed a window with light streaming through it. "As am I, William, but I do not see why you cannot listen."

"I want you." Even as he snapped, William felt the stupidity of it, but could not stop himself. "Charlotte, I am tired of going over this—I want you, and until I have you, I will keep fighting for you."

"Fighting who? Me? Are we at war? Do not try to convince me of your overwhelming affection for me!"

William swore under his breath. This was not how it was meant to happen, not what he intended, but the desire and the need for her tested his patience.

"Look, it is not as though I don't have other options!" He cursed himself the second the words left his mouth.

"Well, that is a relief, for I was concerned you may die alone!" Charlotte shot back. "I knew this was a mistake. I should have gone back inside the Assembly Rooms and listened to Mozart."

Was there a greater fool in the world than he? What had he been thinking? "Wait, Charlotte!"

But she was almost running away. "You do not have to use me to pass the time until you meet another potential conquest, Your Grace. I shall keep you no longer."

He caught up with her, and there was genuine pain across her face. Christ in Heaven, how could he say he cared about her and then wound her within the same breath?

"It is not like that!"

"And I am sure we can find someone prettier, younger, and more charming in the recital," she snapped as they turned the corner. "Give your brother two minutes. He never takes long!"

"Stop!" he said.

It was fortunate for William that there was no one else on the street, for they would have been horrified at the way he grabbed her shoulders and forced her to stop and look at him.

Both breathless from arguing, William fought the desire to crush her into his arms and kiss that argumentative mouth. This was not the time to display his passion. He needed to make this right.

"If you loved me," he said in a voice far calmer than he felt, "then none of this would matter."

Was it his imagination, the way Charlotte avoided his gaze? Or was it merely shyness?

"If you loved me, you would trust me, and a few weeks would be more than enough," he continued in a low voice, dropping his hands from her shoulders.

Charlotte did not speak for a long moment. "I cannot make the promise you want."

She looked torn, genuinely unable to decide, and it pained William far greater than anything had before.

"You do not have to be afraid," he whispered, taking a step toward her, so she tilted her head to keep looking into his eyes. "Ignore Society's gossips. You must get accustomed to receiving attention after fading into the background for so long! Do you truly hide from the fact there may be someone out there who truly cares for you and wants to spend each day of their life with you?"

Charlotte dropped her gaze to her hands. His whole body burned. If she wanted him, if she loved him, then she would know. This was not something in your life you could be unsure of, could it?

William sighed. "God, Charlotte, I want you so badly. But I will not rush you. Your good opinion is something I will continue to seek. I will give you every proof I can of my honesty. Why would I want to speak to other ladies? You are the one who makes my heart sing."

She looked at him, evidently unsure whether to believe him.

Words were not going to be enough. Pulling her into his arms, he placed a reverential kiss on her lips filled with passion and worship.

When the kiss ended, he held her tight. "I mean it, Charlotte. I intend to earn you, even if you cannot see it."

Her eyes were bright. "I do not believe I fully understand you."

"Good," he breathed. "I never understand myself when I am with you."

After several minutes of stolen kisses, he finally released her. "We should return to the recital, or I shall absolutely ruin your reputation."

"Out in the dark, alone, with William the Womanizer?" she teased.

He groaned. "Please do not allow that to become your nickname for me, I could not bear it. Here."

He offered her his arm, and with just a moment of hesitation, she took it. His heart swelled as they walked up the steps into the Assembly Rooms, and they found two seats near the back as the conductor led the musicians into a swelling sonata.

Charlotte was quickly lost by the performance. William hardly remembered a moment of it; he was captivated by her.

CHAPTER ELEVEN

I T WAS THE heat, Charlotte told herself. Sunday had brought the first proper sunshine of the year, and she had not accounted for this in her wardrobe. The organ music rose as the congregation filed into the church.

Her cheeks heated at the memory of those words. Why was she so afraid? Why did she shy away like a wild horse any time William mentioned marriage?

Someone coughed near the back of the church, which she ignored. She had found a seat in a pew near the front, as was befitting her status, and stared at the altar while Reverend Michaels prepared himself.

Was this not exactly what she had wanted, what she had given up hope of ever receiving? Attention from a gentleman? A man, moreover, who was handsome, charming, and titled? Someone who cared for her?

There was another cough from the other side of the pews, but Charlotte did not look around, too overwhelmed by her thoughts.

She swallowed. It always happened without warning, the overwhelming emotions for her mother. Four years. Sometimes she could go an entire week without thinking of her, and all of a sudden, she remembered. If her mother had been alive, she could have asked her for advice. What would she have said? She would have liked William, that was certain.

"Lady Charlotte."

She jumped. The gentleman on whom her thoughts had been so eagerly running was standing right beside her.

He looked dashing in his tailored coat, embroidered waistcoat peeking through. He smiled faintly, and all Charlotte's worries and concerns melted. He did something wild to her, and she was about to return the smile when her gaze shifted.

William was not alone. On one side of him stood his brother, John, waving at someone else. On the other side of him was a young woman—very young. She could only be fifteen or so and dressed in a fine muslin dress with pearls decorating her bonnet.

The girl caught Charlotte's eyes and blushed. Tugging at William's coat sleeve, she whispered something in his ear. Charlotte wanted to turn away, but she seemed unable to. William nodded, and the girl giggled, eyes flashing toward Charlotte.

How dare he. After their conversation just a few nights ago, after she had been so open, so vulnerable! To attend church with a girl young enough to be her daughter.

"Why, Lady Charlotte!"

She blinked and then turned to face him. "Your Grace."

"What a pleasure it is to see you this fine morning," he said.

She swallowed. "Good morning, Your Grace, my lord…miss."

It was impossible to hide the coldness of her tones, and the young woman wilted under Charlotte's gaze.

William looked from one to the other. "I was just saying to Prudence…"

"I cannot believe you," Charlotte said quietly, attempting to keep her voice calm and level. Lady Romeril had just taken the seat beside her. "After all your fine words, here you are with the youngest chit of a girl I have ever seen!"

The girl flushed and glanced at William, who opened his mouth to speak, but Charlotte stopped him.

"I do not want to hear it. I knew you were just waiting for someone prettier and younger, and you have the gall to deny it."

John opened his mouth to speak, but Charlotte would not allow it. She would have her say and then leave. To think she had believed him.

"Well, this foolish girl may have believed your lies, *Your Grace,* but I am through with you. Good day."

The girl looked absolutely mortified. A smile crept over William's face.

"What have you got to smile about?" she inquired coldly. She should leave, she should just walk away, but she couldn't. Something about him kept her here. Some invisible chain between them.

William spoke in a quiet voice. "You are jealous."

"I am not jealous!" she blustered. "I am impressed, I suppose, at how quickly you have overcome your feelings for me."

The words were painful to admit. The girl was still looking terrified, and she moved closer to William as though he would protect her from this madwoman.

Shame mingled with defiance rushed through Charlotte. It was her right to speak her mind, and what did it matter that this girl was in the way?

William leaned down, hesitated, and with a wry look said, "Lady Charlotte, may I introduce you to Prudence. Lady Prudence Lennox, my sister."

Charlotte stared in mortification. "Sister."

He nodded, his grin never disappearing.

The ground cracking open and swallowing her up was the only solution to this situation. Why had she not thought of that? Why did she have to speak before she had taken a moment to think?

"You...you only mentioned Honora," she said uselessly.

He nodded. "Prudence is but fourteen and has come to visit us during the Easter holidays from her school in Kent. Pru, go and find a seat with John, won't you?"

The girl nodded. William's siblings stepped away from him. "You have no reason to be jealous. I spoke the truth when I said you are the only lady I am courting."

Charlotte could feel the heat of his touch through her gown, and in a wild moment, she wanted to throw herself at him, kiss him, and tell him everything was settled between them.

"You must forgive me, William. And apologize to your sister for me. I know it will be hard for her to believe, but I meant her no harm. I was just surprised and find it hard to believe you are in earnest, William. I do not have a high opinion of most gentlemen, and one of my deepest fears is…is that you are teasing me. Jesting with me."

It took courage to admit those dark thoughts, and Charlotte stared at him, looking for any hint of revulsion.

But William's face fell. "Do you actually believe that? Do you truly think so little of me, or yourself?"

It was strange to have such an intimate conversation at the end of a pew in church with countless others milling about, bowing, gossiping, hoping to see and be seen. But Charlotte looked into his eyes and knew she could not run away.

"I do not wish to, but experience has taught me people interested in a woman like me are after something."

"Yes." William nodded seriously. "You."

His hand had not left her arm, and Charlotte suddenly felt the need to escape his touch, to free herself from this anchor.

"You say that so easily," she said quietly. "I am still becoming acquainted with you. It is only a few weeks since we first met."

"You know all the important things about me."

She shook her head. It could not be this simple. "No, there is so much about you I do not know. Your favorite color, piece of music, where you were born, the food you hate."

"Those things do not matter," he said. "What matters is how I feel about you. How we feel about each other. What I do not understand is whether you feel anything for me."

She hesitated. What did she feel for him? How could she translate desire into words? The heat she felt every time he looked at her, how whenever she was in his presence, she never wanted to leave, and when any other woman spoke to him, she wanted to rip her away from him, for William was Charlotte's.

But it was deeper than that. The way he laughed, that lilt in his voice when he thought he was going to say something amusing. The grin he made when someone else did. Every facet of him made her love him more.

It was not *her* feelings she doubted.

She bit her lip. It was time to voice one of the deepest concerns she had, and her cheeks burned to even think it here at church.

"Perhaps…perhaps you merely wish to seduce me."

At the worst possible moment, the organ music rose in volume, and Reverend Michaels started walking down the nave toward the altar.

"Come on," William muttered. His grip on her arm changed, becoming a pull that forced her to her feet.

"What?"

It was clear now that his intention was that she join the Lennox siblings, who almost took up an entire pew on their own. She sat at the end of the pew with William on her right. Lady Prudence was staring at her curiously.

"Good morning, dear friends," Reverend Michaels began with a smile as he gazed at his flock. "And what a wonderful morning it is. As we come together to celebrate the bounty of spring and the coming of summer, we look to God, the Creator…"

"If I merely wished to seduce you," a low whisper spoke into her ear, "then I would have abandoned your company long ago. Charlotte, you are important to me. Our time together is important to me. I was under the impression you enjoyed it, too."

Charlotte clasped her hands tightly in her lap.

"Why would I go to the trouble of introducing my sister to you if I was not serious in my intentions?

She glanced at him. "Intentions?"

"You must think me an awful cad if you do not believe I have greater plans than sitting beside you in church one morning. One day, I would like to meet you at that altar with Reverend Michaels and a few witnesses in attendance."

She would not read more in his words than was already there.

"We will start with hymn number fifty-nine," the reverend directed.

Though she knew the hymn, she made no attempt to sing. How could she? *I am Lady Charlotte St. Maur,* she told herself. *You do not have to do anything, speak to anyone, or do anything unless you want to.*

The church service disappeared in a blur punctuated by moments of accidental intimacy, her hand brushing up against William's as they placed their hymnals back on the pew.

It was almost a relief when Reverend Michaels brought his hands together. "Go in peace to love and serve the Lord."

"We will," Charlotte chorused automatically with the congregation.

John rose quickly. "Pru and I will see you outside, William, do not rush."

They were gone before Charlotte could say anything more in apology to the youngest Lennox.

"John is quite eager that we continue as friends, you know," William said quietly. "Despite any…misunderstandings."

She gave a wry laugh. "Friends? William, I hardly know what that word would mean for us. Friends, acquaintances, lovers, courters? What are we?"

"Ah, Lady Charlotte!"

She sighed. She knew that voice and did not need Lady Romeril casting aspersions rightly or wrongly about the nature of her conversation with William.

"I thought I saw you there," declared Lady Romeril, who pushed her way along the pew. "We barely had a moment to talk before this gentleman wrenched you from me. Good morning, Your Grace, I hope I am not interrupting?"

"Not at all," he said gallantly with a smile. "But you will have to excuse me, Lady Romeril, for I am afraid I am holding my siblings up for their afternoon engagement. Lady Charlotte, I am your servant."

He bowed and kissed her hand. Then he was gone.

Lady Romeril did not wait long to begin again. "I must say, this hot weather is doing absolutely nothing for me. We older ladies must be wary of sudden changes, for it does naught but ill to our health, I am sure you will agree!"

Charlotte stared in disbelief at the woman who was easily twice her age, if not more. *We older ladies?*

"It is certainly a warm day," she said hastily. "I had not expected it to be so warm, with the wind yesterday."

"Ah, but now we can expect warmer weather, and I must change my pelisses," Lady Romeril replied with a smug look. "I have so many, you see. Why, when I last saw the Prince Regent, dear Prinny, I said to him…"

"Yes," Charlotte said without really heeding her words.

"…the Duke of Mercia?"

Charlotte started and saw Lady Romeril staring.

"I said, are you still acting as chaperone for the Duke of Mercia?" Lady Romeril repeated. "I know he is still on the hunt for a bride, for I have seen no announcement. Has he found a suitable lady?"

Charlotte swallowed. It was impossible not to see the irony of the situation. How could she tell one of the matriarchs of the *ton* that it was she who seemed to be receiving his addresses?

"You know," she said slowly. "I think he has."

CHAPTER TWELVE

THIRTY-SIX HOURS. HE had attempted not to count them, but it was impossible. It had been thirty-six hours since he had seen Lady Charlotte St. Maur.

William breathed out slowly to calm his frantically beating heart. It was pathetic, standing out here in the freezing cold night, thinking about how he should have spent every one of those hours with Charlotte, rather than apart from her.

Don't tease me anymore, Charlotte.

It was intolerable, pacing up and down Queen Square. He had been convinced that she was the one for him, the only one.

But he had to be sure. This wasn't France where pretty girls could be wooed within hours and left within minutes.

No, this was Bath, the height of society, and he was a duke now. Taking Lady Charlotte to bed could have consequences. He could barely resist her, and he was almost sure she wanted him. He wanted her. *All of her.*

William stamped his feet as he paused outside Charlotte's house. This was ridiculous If he did not get a move on soon, there was every chance someone would walk by and assume he was there to burgle the place, not pound the door down to get his hands on the lady of the house.

It was now or never. Despite years in the army, some nights more terrible than any man should ever endure, William had never been frightened of entering a battle. Not like this.

But then, he had never had so much to lose.

As though controlled like a puppet on a string, he walked awkwardly up the steps and rang the bell.

He shivered from anticipation as he waited. In mere moments, he would see her again, and if he played his cards right…

The front door opened, and a stern face appeared. "Yes?"

William started. He had not considered Matthews intimidating before, but he stood as though guarding the gates of heaven. And wasn't he?

"Good evening, Matthews," he managed to say. "Is Lady Charlotte at home?"

Damn fool of a question. It was almost ten o'clock in the evening, long past visiting hours. What did he think he was doing?

The butler clearly agreed with William's internal thoughts. Eyebrows raised, he opened the door to allow him inside. "Lady Charlotte is not receiving visitors," he said smoothly, shutting the front door and bowing. "I fail to understand why you require a visit with my lady at this late hour," he said baldly.

William drew himself up to his full height and saw with dismay that it still did not match Matthews.

"Because I love her." The statement was short, true, but he had spoken honestly and without guile.

Matthews raised an eyebrow. "Indeed."

William waited, but the butler said nothing. The conversation rather falling on its feet, he continued, "I would like to tell her so, Matthews, and I found I could not sleep without her knowing."

The butler regarded him for a moment and then said quietly, "I have sworn to protect her. I promised her mother that I would keep an eye on her until she married, and she had another to keep her safe."

It was the last thing William had expected, and from a butler no less! But now he regarded Matthews properly. He saw an elderly gentleman who had likely seen Charlotte grow from a small child into a woman.

"I am not here to hurt her," he said. "But need her to know I am serious about my suit, and it is my wish to marry her. Lady Charlotte will become the Duchess of Mercia if I have any say in the matter."

"Her Grace?" It was clear that Matthews greatly approved of the title for his charge. "Well then, that is different. You are in earnest?"

"Never more so," William said truthfully.

The butler frowned at him, during which William felt an overwhelming urge to fidget, but he resisted.

"The lady of this house, before Lady Charlotte," said the butler finally, "always wished to see her daughter married."

"If Lady Charlotte will have me, I would marry her within the week."

Matthews smiled. "If she married anyone, it would not be within a week. Your Grace, may I take your coat?"

William tried to prevent his shoulders from sagging with visible relief as the servant took his coat, gloves, and hat.

"One moment, sir. Who shall I say is calling?"

William grinned at the gentle cheek from the butler. He knew full well who William was. But then an idea crept into his mind. "Tell her a friend is in need of a chaperone."

It truly was a glare from the butler this time, but Matthews did not say another word. Turning on his heels, he walked out of the room, leaving William alone.

The hallway was sparsely lit with only one candle burning. William bit his lip as a clock chimed somewhere in the house. What did he think he was doing, turning up at her door at this time, hoping to be allowed in?

It was scandalous, and no lady of good breeding would ever allow it. He would not blame her if she sent him away. She had her own reputation to protect, after all.

Since that moment in the alley—no, before then, when he had first seen her at her brother's wedding and decided to follow her—he had wanted more. Charlotte's face had been seared into his mind, and he could not get rid of her.

William moved about the hallway restlessly. How many chits, just girls really, had he been introduced to in that time? Ten? Fifteen? Maybe even twenty, but none of them compared. He had not given them a thought once they left his presence.

There was only one woman for him. He had been conquered by her without her even knowing it, without trying. Wasn't that part of the attraction? She had spoken to him coldly, angrily, without interest, and he had warmed to her.

Every taste of you makes me want you more. I cannot take this much longer.

God, he had not realized how true those words were until days without her. He had been convinced that kiss in the lane would make her accept his proposal. Their conversation in church had lifted his hopes only to dash them again. It was time for something drastic.

A door opened, and Matthews came back into the hallway, and this time, there was a knowing smile on his face.

"My Lady Charlotte says," he intoned with a sharp look at William, "she will see you in the study. Second door on the left."

She wanted him. His whole body clenched as he walked to the door. Did she know the signals she was giving?

William tasted blood. He had bitten his lip so hard, he had made it bleed. Was he truly ready for this?

Charlotte. Her name made him shiver all over. With purpose and certainty, William reached out and opened the door.

There she was, just as he had imagined her. Standing by the fire, book in hand, dressed in a nightgown barely covered by a thin dressing gown, reaching for the bell.

William's jaw fell open. It was as though, once again, she had walked straight from his mind and into the world.

"Charlotte," he breathed.

She looked up and yelped at the sight of him, her book sliding to the floor.

"William!" she said, quite evidently shocked to see him. "You must not–I am not dressed for–Matthews said someone needed a chaperone…"

Her voice trailed away as she became conscious of her apparel. William grinned. It was impossible to be more delighted. He had always wondered what had been underneath those drab gowns, and now he knew. A body so delectable, he wondered how he had managed to keep his lips and teeth away from her for so long. A slender waist and rounded breasts. Long legs waiting to encircle him. Waiting for him. Ready for him.

"I did not know that…" She did not seem able to form full sentences as she pulled her dressing gown around her more tightly. "I was ringing the bell for Danvers to bring some clothes down from my room–when Matthews said… chaperone…"

Her splutters did not distract him from noticing the faint flush in her cheeks, the way she looked at him in shock but also in delight. By God, she wanted him as much as he wanted her. She just did not have the words to express it.

William nodded and stepped forward. "At this rate, Charlotte, it'll be you that needs a chaperone."

She took a step back, her eyes wide. "You cannot be serious— William, you cannot be here! What if someone saw you?"

"Nobody saw me."

"You cannot possibly know that for certain. Matthews saw you!"

William shrugged. "I wanted to see you, and I care not who knows. I am not ashamed about the way I feel for you."

Silence fell, and he wondered whether he had gone too far. By God, but he owed Matthews more than a guinea for allowing him into this room—the old butler must be more of a man of the world than he had estimated.

But Charlotte was not easily persuaded, fully aware of her worth and value. Who in her position would permit him to stride into her home and make love to her?

She stared, arms folded across her chest, clearly thinking hard. If she didn't accept him, there was no point. He would rather leave than make her feel coerced.

Charlotte sighed, and William's heart sank.

"You...you have come all this way," she said quietly. "You may as well stay for a drink." She gestured to the nearby cabinet.

William's stomach roiled uncomfortably. Was that just politeness? One drink and then be off with you? Or was that, have a drink and then another, and stay here until the early hours?

"Aren't you going to have one?"

Charlotte shook her head. "I never touch the stuff. Well, except once."

A smile crept over her face without embarrassment. William's curiosity piqued.

"You will have to tell me about it," he said easily, stepping over to the bottles and helping himself to a small portion of port. It would not do to completely lose his head. It was best he remained sober this evening, so every sweet memory—or painful moment—could be remembered.

Holding his drink carefully, William sat on the sofa, hoping Charlotte would join him. She hesitated, standing by the fire, her eyes flickering over the various seating options in the room.

All she needed was a little encouragement, permission to be reckless. He patted the seat beside him, and after a moment's thought, she lowered herself onto the sofa, as far from him as possible. William sighed internally. He had an uphill battle ahead of him.

"There is a story there," he said breezily, leaning back.

Charlotte frowned. "Where?"

"In your smile. In your comment about one drink, and one drink only. I have to say it is not a surprise, considering what you said about your father."

That's the way to seduce a woman. Remind her about her horrific father.

"As you have probably guessed, there is a weakness for alcohol in my family, and so my brother and I vowed we would never touch the stuff."

"And yet, you did. Once."

She laughed and finally met his gaze. "Yes, three months ago. Richard had a misunderstanding with Tabitha. When he believed he had lost her, he consumed a fair bit of whiskey. When I discovered him here in this very study, I took it upon myself to remove immediate temptation from him." She laughed again. "I drank two whole glasses to prevent him from doing so. I must say, I do not see the attraction of a liquid that burns your throat and stomach."

He snorted at the thought of Charlotte tipping her head back and draining the glasses. "I cannot imagine it!"

William saw her shoulders relax. It was wonderful, sitting here, laughing together—as if this was their home.

William swallowed. As Charlotte laughed, part of her dressing gown had become undone, and he had a rather fetching view of the curve of her breast. The view was doing rather uncomfortable things to parts of his body.

"Thank goodness they reconciled," Charlotte said. "I may have developed a serious problem!"

At these words, her laughter subsided, and sadness washed across her features.

"What are you thinking?"

"It is nothing," she said hastily.

"Now, do not do that with me." William raised his glass to his lips, took a sip, and lowered it to his lap. "I think you and I have shared too much to be false with each other. Talk to me. What took you from happiness to misery in a few seconds?"

Charlotte's eyes met his, and there was such intensity William fell silent.

"It is foolish," she said in a quiet voice.

"Nothing you feel is ever foolish."

She smiled weakly. "You are a very charming man, aren't you, William?"

For the first time, he knew what it was to care more for another than himself. "Only with you. Everything I say to you is the truth, I swear it."

They looked at each other in silence.

"It is not much of a secret, after all," she said quietly. "I am sure there are plenty of ladies who feel this way. It is...well, my brother Richard and I were always so close. Close in age, close in temperament. He had vowed never to marry—yes, that is another story—and it was clear there would be few suitors knocking at the door for my hand. I thought he and I would grow old together, prepare Stonehaven Lacey for another family."

Charlotte looked at her hands twisted together in her lap.

"Then?" William prompted.

"Then he met Tabitha. Do not misunderstand me, they are perfect for each other. I never thought I would meet a match for my brother, and when he did, I realized how selfish I was. I wanted him to be happy, but I also wanted him to be happy with me. He is married now, and they have gone to Stonehaven Lacey to prepare for their own family, and I..."

William watched her, saw the way she delicately chose her words, how she hesitated, made sure each sentence did not betray her feelings too deeply. But she did not need to. He could see the pain in her, the disappointment, and the shame she felt.

"It was easier to come to Bath," Charlotte said finally. "I was made welcome at Stonehaven Lacey, but it is their home. They did not need a third person there."

She finished in obvious embarrassment. He could not take his eyes from her. She felt things so deeply, rarely sharing those thoughts. The way she was speaking, he guessed she had never shared these particular thoughts, this specific pain.

"I never had to think about such things," he said quietly, "and in some ways, I think it is a blessing. I was not raised to this sort of life, and I do not fit into the nobility the way you do. Born to it. Raised to it."

She snorted and shook her head. "William, you are the Duke of Mercia."

"Madness, isn't it? No, honestly, Charlotte, you cannot imagine in turn what it is like to grow up a normal lad in a middling family, work hard all your life, and then be told by letter, you have a title waiting for you."

She leaned forward. "How could you have a title waiting for you? I must admit, I have been curious for a while. Wasn't your father…"

"You said so yourself, you and your brother were preparing Stonehaven Lacey for another family," he pointed out. "And it happens, does it not? The male line ends in one branch of the family, and another rises to take its place. My mother was cast off for marrying a solider. She never spoke of her family. We just thought they were against the old war, hated the army, you know. It was not until we received the news that my uncle, her brother, had died that we realized what a life my mother had left behind. All for love."

William hoped his hint at love would provoke a response.

Charlotte scrunched her nose. "It does not seem possible you did not know at all. Surely her name would have given you an idea."

"When you are a child, you believe what you are told," he said. "I never thought much about my mother's maiden name, and I never thought to ask."

"Perhaps that is why you are so bored with those children you keep getting introduced to."

William laughed. Now, this was another side of Charlotte he loved. He loved her. Every part of her, the serious side, the playful side, and the contemplative side. Each part contributed to who she was.

"Bored?" He set down the glass of port, hardly touched. "Charlotte, I have had far too much fun with you to be bored."

He had resisted for so long but could not restrain himself any longer. He leaned forward to kiss her.

She leaned back at first, but as their eyes met, she shivered and moved forward. As soon as their lips met, she moaned, giving in to the kiss.

William groaned and brought his arms around her, pulling her to him as tightly as he could. It was glorious. Before his mind could even conceive of what to do next, they were both lying on the sofa, her dressing gown open, and nothing but her nightgown and his shirt between them.

William lost himself in her lips. He wanted to explore them, know them, possess them. For several minutes, all he could focus on was her face, mouth, and the kiss that burned his lips, making him hungry for more.

Eventually, he broke the kiss to say the words in his heart.

"I love you, Charlotte."

"Do you, indeed?"

"I would never lie to you, nor about something so important," he said slowly. He had to get this right. He would only have one chance. "You know," he said shakily, "I have actually asked you to marry me twice."

"You never actually asked," Charlotte countered, her hair wild across the sofa and her lips red from their passion. "You just told me you wanted to, which I do not think counts."

William laughed. "Perhaps I am saving it for a special occasion."

"Does this count?"

"Not yet," he growled and lowered his face once more to hers.

The kisses were deepening, and he knew if he did not say something now, he would forever regret it.

He pulled away from her and almost smiled at the small moan of disappointment she made.

"Charlotte, I have to ask, I want more with you."

Her cheeks were flushed and her eyes wide. "More? More of this, you mean, kissing?"

William swallowed. Her fear of being seduced was ringing through his memory. How could he possibly explain it?

"You were wrong when you suspected me of only wanting your company for your body," he said slowly, not taking his gaze from her face, "but you were also right. I would greatly enjoy seducing you. Have you…have you ever considered allowing a gentleman to teach you the ways of pleasure?"

Charlotte hesitated. "Once. It was a long time ago. He was a tutor for our neighbors here in Bath." It was not the answer he had expected, and it must have shown on his face, because she laughed. "Nothing happened, really. A few stolen kisses behind the curtains as I visited to watch the music lesson."

"Charlotte St. Maur, you minx!" William could hardly contain himself. He was pleased. "And you wanted more?"

There was a hint of embarrassment on her face but no shame. "He did. I did not consider one and twenty a good age to lose one's innocence and reputation, when marriage—I thought—was so close. Now I look back with a few regrets."

"Regrets?"

She nodded. "I could have experienced something beautiful, I think. Something that I will now never know."

There was a knowing sparkle in her eyes that made William's heart leap. She could not have been plainer if she had spoken the words aloud.

He knew exactly what he wanted to do, and he knew she would let him. She was ready. William leaned forward to worship her mouth, his right hand untangled itself from her wild mane and slowly made its way down her body.

It met with continuous temptation, her breasts, quivering under the slightest touch, those hips so round and soft. But eventually, his hand reached that secret, warm, delicious place where he wanted to sink his manhood right now—but not yet. He had so much more pleasure to give.

"Charlotte," he managed in a shaky voice. "Do you trust me?"

She looked at him with wide eyes hazy with desire and nodded—and cried out with pleasure as he slipped two of his fingers inside her.

William almost cried out with her. God's teeth, but she was ready for him. Her nightgown was damp, and she tightened around his fingers. As he moved them gently, he caressed that nub of pleasure, and she arched against the sofa.

"William!"

Hearing his name cried out was enough to push him over the edge, but he gritted his teeth. This was not the time to lose control. This was when he could show Charlotte exactly what she meant to him. How she deserved to be loved.

Lowering his mouth to her neck, he teased kisses down it until he reached her décolletage without forgetting to keep his fingers moving ever so gently, working up to a rhythm, slowly, slowly.

But she did not want slowly. She twitched with desire and moaned, eventually managing to whisper, "More, William."

It was too much. Burying his face in her breasts and finding her nipple with his tongue, William caressed and stroked, her panting and moans echoing in his ears and driving him wild as he brought her to climax.

Her spasms around his fingers made his manhood desperate to be inside her. As she settled, she looked into his eyes with shock and surprise.

"That was…wonderful."

"And there is more," he whispered, unable to stop himself from kissing her again. "More, Charlotte, and I want to give it to you."

She gazed at him in wonder, and as he opened his mouth to ask her once and for all to make him happy and marry him, she leaned and kissed him full on the mouth.

"In that case," she said, "why don't you come upstairs with me?"

CHAPTER THIRTEEN

F OR A HEART-STOPPING instant, Charlotte could not believe what she had just said. Lying on the sofa almost completely naked with a man—who could have believed it?

She would not have believed it even an hour ago, and yet here she was. And here he was.

William Lennox, Duke of Mercia. How could one man mean so much to her? Just looking at him made her melt.

In that case, why don't you come upstairs with me?

She trusted him. How could she not? He was an honorable man, one with a deep sense of pride in himself and his word. Charlotte was sure he would not tell anyone about tonight. Her reputation was safe with him.

He had come here tonight wanting this—wanting her. It had been obvious the moment he entered the room.

She wanted more of that divine pleasure he had given her, pleasure beyond what was possible on this earth.

But he had not responded to her offer. In fact, William was gazing at her with complete astonishment. Had she gone too far? He will end up marrying someone else, to be sure. Any man gets bored of chasing one woman eventually. But would he give her this? Would he give her tonight?

"We would be taking a risk."

"I will not tell anyone," she whispered. "I trust you. I know you will not, either."

He swallowed. "But...but what about a child?"

Pushing him away, she walked around the sofa to a small, unassuming wooden box placed in the corner of the room on a table. She opened it and pulled out a preservative.

William sat up hurriedly. "Why in God's name do you have a French letter?"

She laughed at the way he responded. One would almost think he had never seen one before, and that man was far too good with his hands to be so innocent. "They are not mine! They are Richard's."

His eyes widened, and Charlotte explained, "Look, we are both of age, and he and I have always been honest with each other. He has no secrets from me. I knew he had women here, and he was determined after taking his vow never to marry. So, shall we?"

Rising from the sofa and jumping over it, he pulled her into his arms and a deep kiss.

When they finally broke apart, neither had much breath, but William managed to say, "Yes."

He was hers, and she was very soon to be his. It was easy to lose yourself in those blue eyes, and she did not want to break the silence.

But something hot and fiery was stirring inside her, and she could not delay.

Taking him by the hand, she moved toward the door and opened it quietly, looking into the corridor to find no one. Matthews must be giving the servants their orders for tomorrow.

Something was making a rhythmic sound, and it took a moment to realize it was the sound of her own heart thumping in her ears. It was difficult to believe this was real. She had a gentleman at home, and she had invited him to her bedchamber—and what was more, he had accepted. She was about to do what the most scandalous ladies in society did.

Pulling him quietly through the doorway, it did not take more than a minute to creep up the staircase and into her bedroom. She pulled him through the door and shut it quietly behind her.

William stood in the center of the room, and Charlotte swallowed. She had never been more vulnerable, more alone. No man had ever been in her bedchamber. Her childhood paintings were on the walls, and some rather racy novels by Mrs. Radcliffe were by the side of the bed. Several pairs of stockings, all in need of mending, were scattered around. Charlotte colored.

But William was not looking around at her room. He was staring at her with hungry eyes.

So, this how it felt before you were bedded for the first time. She had not expected so much fear and anticipation, but the memory of pleasure was still recent, and she shivered at the thought of it.

She moved soundlessly to the bed and placed the preservative on her bedside table. Without looking, she whispered, "You have...have done this before."

"Sneaked into your bedroom? No."

She turned around with a fierce look, and William's grin softened. He walked toward her, kissed her lightly on the lips, and hesitated.

"Yes," he said finally. "After a battle, you do anything, anything you can to feel alive."

She nodded. In this moment, she did not care. He was here with her now. That was what mattered. "I have not felt alive in years."

With shaking fingers but absolute determination, she allowed her dressing gown to fall to the floor. Before she could absorb the look of astonishment on William's face, her fingers found the ribbon fastenings of her nightgown and allowed that to fall, too.

For a shimmering instant, she stood there, completely naked, her eyes fixed on William. The temptation to cover herself with her hands came and went. She wanted him to see all of her. All she could hope was that he liked what he saw.

William growled and closed the distance between them, pulling her into his arms and kissing her wildly. Charlotte clung to him, clung to him as though he was the only real thing in the world—and in that instant, he was.

"I promised you pleasure," William panted, breaking apart with great effort, "and I meant that."

Charlotte's arms were around him, and she frowned to have them pulled away. He pulled at his shirt, unbuttoning it quickly and dropping it to the floor. His boots were next, then breeches, and then he was standing before her just as naked as she was.

She gasped. He was even more masculine than she could have imagined, all chiseled peaks and curling hair.

"Do not be afraid," he said softly.

"I am not."

"Call me, Will."

"Yes."

"Is this a good time to ask you to marry me?"

Before she could reply, he picked her up and threw her on the bed. She fell back into the softness and did not have time to think or say anything before he had joined her, covering her body with his own.

Charlotte gasped. This was unfathomable, the sensation of his skin on hers, the closeness, the way her fingers could explore—nervously at first, then with greater certainty.

"You should be careful," she breathed, "or I may actually take you up on that offer."

Her heart was racing, but she knew this was all a part of the experience, the words of love, the proposal of marriage. He was here to woo her, and she wanted that, but he could not, surely, be serious about his offer.

William kissed her deeply, and her whole body melted.

"I think," he said between kisses down her neck, "I will make it my mission this night to make you say yes."

Charlotte hardly knew what she was saying, her body was so alive.

"I will not."

William raised his head. There was a spark of a challenge in his eyes as he said, "Oh, really?"

She should have expected it, but this exquisite pleasure was so new, she simply could not control herself as his hand moved once more to her secret place. Sinking his fingers into her, he nibbled at her neck and whispered in her ear.

"Say yes."

Charlotte squirmed, desperate for his fingers to move inside her, to stroke her to that wonderful ecstasy once more, but she would not give in. Even with all this pleasure.

"No—oh, Will!"

His fingers made her cry out as his tongue worshiped her neck. The sensation rippled through her body.

"Say yes," he moaned into her soft flesh. "God, Charlotte, say yes."

"No," she whispered, her hips bucking against his magic fingers.

She wanted to cry out, scream out his name until he brought her to ecstasy, but she couldn't. Matthews and the other servants would hear them, and the thought of being discovered nude and entangled with a gentleman—a gentleman, moreover, who was pleasuring her with both his mouth and his fingers—made her writhe against the blankets.

"Marry me," he groaned as he raised his head to look into her eyes. "Christ, Charlotte, marry me!"

"No," she panted, "no, no, no!"

It was all too much, and William cried out in frustration as he dipped his head once more to kiss her breasts, his fingers flickering wildly inside her as she felt that buildup of ecstasy once more, and she exploded around him.

"Will!" Charlotte cried, and she did not attempt to keep her voice quiet. The pleasure was overwhelming.

When she opened her eyes, there was a rueful look on his face.

"You did not say yes."

Charlotte reveled in her power over this man, who made her feel the most unbelievable sensations. She smiled knowingly.

"By God," William breathed. "You are the one in charge here, not me. But I will get that yes."

Before she could think about what he was doing, so lulled was she by her recent climax, William nestled himself between her legs and reached over for the preservative.

"Will," she said quietly. "Are you sure?"

"Surer than I have been about anything," he said, placing it over himself.

It did not seem possible that he would fit inside her.

He was sure; he plunged into her.

It was tight at first, too tight, and she squirmed at the discomfort, but William understood. Leaning on his elbows, he kissed her slowly and devotedly while one hand stroked her neck, moving tantalizingly close to her breasts but never quite reaching them.

His lips on hers and the gentleness of his hands made her feel safe. As she relaxed, her body softened, and his manhood slid deeper into her.

It was a wondrous feeling. She could never have imagined feeling this close with someone.

"This is…" She couldn't finish the thought.

He nodded. "Now you can see why I wanted this so badly with you. I wanted to be one with you, to give you pure pleasure. Not another man."

"Another man?" Charlotte asked. "You are the only one for me."

He moaned at her words and pulled himself out of her almost completely, leaving just the tip of himself inside her. "Now tell me you'll marry me, Charlotte. Tell me yes. That's all I need from you."

No matter how experienced he was, how much of the world he knew, she was the one in control. "No."

His blue eyes darkened. "Well, then. You will have to be punished until you give me the answer I need."

William entered her again, and this time, Charlotte arched her back. *Punishment?* If he thought this was punishment, she would hate to see pleasure.

She gasped as he began a ruthless rhythm, slow at first but deeper than she thought possible. His hand pleasured her breasts as his tongue pleasured her mouth, and all she could do was cry out until he whispered into her ear.

"Say yes."

"No," she breathed.

"Please," he said, his voice breaking as he begged. "Please, Charlotte, say yes."

Something wild was starting to overwhelm her, and it was like when he made her explode with his fingers but deeper, across her whole body. She never wanted to be without him again.

He thrust into her faster and faster, and suddenly, Charlotte could do nothing, think nothing, just feel because her body was shattering in pleasure.

"Yes!"

CHAPTER FOURTEEN

W ILLIAM CLASPED THE wonderful woman to him and sighed.
By God, he could never have hoped for this.

As they lay together naked, nestled under a blanket, it was difficult to take it in. Beautiful, intelligent, witty, wonderful company, and a woman he could talk to for hours and never tire of. And here she was, in his arms, after she had welcomed him to her bed.

Charlotte breathed contentedly, her eyes closed, and William tightened his grip.

"To think most men have to propose months before enjoying such pleasure," he said softly.

She laughed, and his manhood twitched. But William quelled those particular thoughts. This was new to her, and it would not do to wear her out this early. Not now that he had offered her marriage, and she had finally accepted.

"To tell the truth," she whispered. "I do not consider my yes an acceptance of your proposal. It was hardly fair, you must admit. No lady can be held accountable for what she says while teased...that way."

William's heart sank. *Ah.* In that case, his hopes for her and their life together weren't exactly fixed. She had not said yes to his proposal, but then, she had not said no. To be sure, she had moaned no several times, and the thought of it made him slightly hard again, but she had not pushed him away.

"I must ask then," he said, his hand stroking her back, "what circumstances will I need for you to say yes and mean it?"

She did not speak for several minutes but placed her hand on his chest and considered her fingers. Eventually, she said, "I do not know. I always wanted to marry when I was young."

"You are young."

Charlotte snorted. "Five and thirty? You are kind to lie to me. No, when I was a young debutante entering into society, all I could think of was marriage. As I grew older and became more ignored, that dream faded. When I was first asked to act as a chaperone, that was when I knew the dream had died. No one marries the chaperone, not even you."

"But I want to," he said seriously.

She stretched and curled back into his arms. "I have said goodbye to that dream. It seems strange, attempting to resurrect it after so long."

"Did it truly die? It wasn't...sleeping? Waiting for the right gentleman?"

Her entire life was shaped around helping others to court and wed. When did Charlotte get her turn?

"Perhaps it just needs encouragement," Charlotte said.

William laughed. "And tonight has not been encouragement enough?"

"A woman of five and thirty..."

"Oh, hang five and thirty," said William with a touch of annoyance. She looked at him with surprise. "Yes, blast it, I say. I do not care how old you are, what does it matter to me? If I had met you before now, years ago, I would not have the title, and our lives would have been completely different. I doubt we would have met at all."

"I would have at least looked once."

Overwhelmed by affection, William kissed her on the nose and said more seriously, "I mean it, Charlotte. I want to marry you, and if you are not careful, I will go to your brother and ask his permission."

She scrunched her nose in that endearing way that said she had heard something she did not quite like. "Richard would never be fool enough to give his permission unless I gave mine."

"I would wait. I would wait and win you both over."

He had never expected to make such a declaration to a woman, and what's more, he meant it. There was something intensely fragile about Charlotte St. Maur. No one else seemed to have noticed.

Charlotte smiled. "I will bear that in mind. But right now, all I want to do is sleep."

She tucked her head into his neck and sighed deeply.

"I should go," he said wearily, not wishing to leave her, but knowing honor demanded it. "The last thing your reputation needs is for a gentleman to be found here when your lady's maid comes in tomorrow morning."

Charlotte's eyes were closed, and her arms tightened around him. "You are right. You should go."

William chuckled. "Charlotte, you are not making this easy for me."

"I don't intend to," came the sleepy reply.

She had become everything to him, and they had shared everything together. He was determined to have her accept his proposal before the week was out.

So, what did it matter? William nestled into her welcoming arms and allowed sleep to overtake him.

CHAPTER FIFTEEN

W HEN CHARLOTTE OPENED her eyes, there was a smile on her face.

She was also completely naked.

The memories of the previous night came flooding back. Such pleasure. Such closeness. Intimacy she could never have hoped for, never imagined.

As the soft morning light found its way around the thick curtains, those memories seemed a dream. Almost too good to be true. But they were true, and he was her duke, William Lennox, the Duke of Mercia.

Charlotte shifted and luxuriated in being completely naked in her bed. There was nothing quite like the feeling of linen sheets against her skin. How would she ever wear a nightgown in bed again?

I mean it, Charlotte. I want to marry you, and if you are not careful, I will go to your brother and ask his permission.

It was difficult to believe her daring, but she would never regret it. It had been her chance, her one opportunity to experience making love. She may never marry, but she would always have that knowledge.

The other side of the bed was empty. William must have left in the early hours, allowing her to sleep and giving him the chance to sneak out without prying eyes. What would the gossips of Bath have said if they had seen the dashing new duke—only recently entering polite society—leaving the house of a known spinster?

After several minutes of thinking, she pulled herself out of bed. Her nightgown and dressing gown looked forlorn lying there on the floor abandoned.

It had been glorious when she had allowed them to fall to the floor. Charlotte laughed aloud at the memory of William's face. His jaw had tightened, and his eyes had drunk her in. Exactly the reaction she had hoped for.

"Hours ago," she whispered to the empty room. "And everything has changed."

She glanced into her looking glass. There was no difference in her looks. Fine lines around her eyes and a few hairs silvery rather than chestnut.

But there was something different. Was it the way she held herself? Something felt different, as though she had crossed a bridge previously barred. She had joined that exclusive group of women who had experienced the loving touch of a man.

What a man. Charlotte shivered at the recollection of his naked form. She had studied classical art, naturally, and knew in theory what to expect—but he had been more.

She dressed and rushed down the stairs and did not wait for the footman outside the breakfast room to open the door for her. The table had been laid and was waiting for her, despite the late hour, and there was a letter waiting.

"Good morning, my lady." With the uncanny knack of the best butlers, Matthews appeared in the room without seeming to have taken a step.

Charlotte beamed, and Matthews raised an eyebrow.

"It is good to see you in such a pleasant mood, my lady," he said smoothly, pulling out the chair. "A letter came early for you."

"Thank you." Charlotte poured a steaming hot cup of tea. "That will be all."

Accustomed to Charlotte's wish of breakfasting alone, he bowed out of the room and closed the door quietly.

Charlotte sipped the tea and sighed. Nothing was the same; even tea was different! Was there a sweetness there that hadn't been there before? Was this how the rest of her life was going to be?

Only after she buttered two pieces of toast and applied marmalade liberally to one of them, did she take another look at the envelope. It was small and discrete with a seal on the back.

A seal she recognized.

A magpie, beak open, around a swirled M. Her heart pounding, Charlotte broke the seal as carefully as she could and unfolded the letter.

Her pulse quickened as she glanced down and saw the elaborate M at the end of the letter. It was a short letter, barely more than a few lines, but she read it slowly, absorbing every word.

My Lady Charlotte,

I would appreciate your company today at twelve o'clock. If this is convenient for you, then please meet me on Pulteney Bridge, where I will be waiting for you. If not convenient, cancel whatever plans you have made.

Mercia

Charlotte glanced at the clock. It was almost eleven o'clock. She still had plenty of time to breakfast, get dressed, and make her way to the Sydney Gardens.

She picked up the teacup but had to immediately place it down because her hand was shaking. In an hour, she would see Will again. She grabbed her toast and ran for the stairs.

If only the clocks would go faster, no, slower!

"Danvers!" she called.

Her lady's maid rushed into the room, never having heard Charlotte shout so loud before. "Yes, my lady?"

Charlotte dropped onto the bed and covered her face with both hands. "You know that new style of ringlets around the face you have wished to attempt for a few months now?"

Removing her hands from her eyes, she saw Danvers's face light up. "The one Miss Tilbury has made so popular?"

Charlotte nodded, heart racing. "I would like to look...beautiful for an engagement this afternoon. I think it is time."

The lady's maid's gaze slipped to her wardrobe. "Are you sure, my lady? You have waited so long."

It was true. Charlotte took a deep breath and hoped she was making the right decision. "I have waited, Danvers, you are right. I think it is time."

The servant stepped across the room eagerly and pulled open the wardrobe door. "My lady, you will not regret it, this gown is just beautiful, and a classic style that has not aged a day since your mother ordered it."

Since your mother chose it. Charlotte had to force herself to stand still as Danvers moved around her like a butterfly, helping her into the last gown her mother had chosen for her. It was a delicate, light blue satin, the tucks under the bust still just as fashionable as when it had been first ordered.

"I have never asked, my lady," Danvers said quietly as she adjusted a loose thread on the hem, "why you have never worn this gown. Indeed, you have refused to even put it on in the years I have known you."

Charlotte took a deep breath. "Just before my mother died, I confided in her my fear...my fear that I would never wed." *She would not allow the tears to come, not now. Not on such a joyful day.* "She listened and comforted me, and the very next day, she ordered this gown. When it arrived, she told me it was the gown my future husband would see me in and know, absolutely, that he had made the right decision."

Saying the words aloud made her smile. *Her husband.* Well, he had not proposed marriage yet, but what else could his letter mean?

"Oh, my lady." Danvers straightened up and smiled sadly. "That is the most beautiful story I have ever heard. I wish you joy."

"We have not announced," Charlotte spluttered. "I mean…Danvers, let us not talk about it anymore. My hair and perhaps a little rouge?"

Charlotte remembered ruefully why she had gotten out of the habit of beautifying herself; it took so long and was more than a little uncomfortable.

But today, of all days, it was worth it. Charlotte bit her lip. *This was starting to overwhelm her, this anticipation of seeing Will again. After sharing such an incredible night, a moment of exquisite passion that she had never known before, what did he want from her today? Could it be he wished to ask her to marry him in seriousness?*

Charlotte breathed out slowly as she placed the bonnet on her head. *This was ridiculous.* She would drive herself mad with wondering, and it was a quarter to twelve. It was time to leave.

The front door snapped shut behind her, and she shivered in the cool breeze rustling the budding branches along the street. A few people had ventured from their homes, umbrellas on their arms, despite the threatening rainclouds.

She walked quickly, passing people in her rapid journey and nodding politely, without giving the opportunity for conversation. She could make out Pulteney Bridge, and there stood a gentleman waiting for her.

William.

Overwhelmed by the desire to run and kiss him, she fought the urge and slowed her pace. It would not do to arrive breathless, without the ability to say a single word.

"I hope I am not late," she smiled nervously as she approached. "I slept in this morning."

He removed his top hat and beamed. Charlotte melted. There was no other gentleman like this.

How had she found such a man, or rather, how had he found her?

It seemed impossible, and as she looked at him, handsome in his well-tailored greatcoat, she wondered what he was doing with her. Past her prime and with little to recommend her, save a title, no other gentleman had ever sought her company.

"You look absolutely beautiful," he said softly.

Her blush was involuntary. "Thank you."

He stared at her, and she laughed.

"My apologies, I just—shall we?"

She nodded. "Yes."

Charlotte moved to accept the arm she assumed would be offered. But it was not. He was a few steps ahead of her before she caught up, discomfort twisting her stomach. Why had he not offered her his arm?

"I have not seen that gown before."

"No, this is new. One that no one has seen."

The Sydney Gardens was almost deserted, with one other couple promenading along its path. Older than them, perhaps in their late forties, with two sullen boys in their wake.

"I never usually put any thought into the clothes I wear," she said. "What does it matter? No one was looking at me."

"I am always looking at you," he countered, a wolfish grin on his face. "But if you ask me, the clothes get in the way."

Her cheeks flushed, and although the other couple was yards from them, her eyes darted to them, concerned they may have heard his words.

"Charlotte," he said, "I am grateful you have met me today. I have not been able to stop thinking about you."

She dropped her gaze. "It has only been a few hours since we have last…seen each other."

"Each moment has been torment."

It was all too much, more a dream than reality. How could this be happening? How could these words of affection be directed at her?

Before saying another word, William stopped and took her arm.

All thought of being seen was forgotten as Charlotte's body responded to his closeness, and her heart responded to his words. He was all she wanted.

"I cannot wait," he whispered, his eyes never leaving hers, "to tell people about our engagement."

Engagement? He had not asked anything of the sort—at least, only in jest or lust.

Now tell me you'll marry me, Charlotte. Tell me yes. That's all I need from you.

She swallowed, her throat dry. "I do not think you have actually...proposed."

William took a step back. "My God, Charlotte. What did you think last night was? Or was it all a jest to you?"

Was it time to admit to herself, as well as him, that she had fallen in love?

"I know your intentions, but I think you will find, Your Grace," she said, attempting to keep her wild thoughts under control, "a proper proposal, one from someone of your class and breeding, includes going somewhere public, where it will be most embarrassing if the intended responds in the negative, getting down on bended knee, and professing their love publicly. I cannot recall *you* ever doing such a thing."

Her eyes met his gaze. They were dark, staring intensely. Had she gone too far?

"My dear, Lady Charlotte," he said in a low voice, stepping toward her, "we made love last night."

Heat seared her cheeks as she leaned away. "That does not equate to a proposal!"

"I thought you loved me when you welcomed me into your bed, and I certainly left it in love with you."

Will grinned and offered his arm, which Charlotte took with a smile. Playing with fire? She had stepped into the flames, and if she was not careful, she would soon be burned, branded with the force of his feelings. Feelings she barely understood.

"I am not saying that I feel differently," she managed to say.

"In that case," he said more seriously as they turned a corner, "tell me, honestly. Is that what it will take?"

"Take?"

"To secure your hand."

Charlotte stared in amazement.

"Is that what you are waiting for?"

"You ask intimate questions," she stated.

"Only the questions which truly matter to me."

She considered him and saw nothing but truth on his face. This man had suffered through battle and watched men die violently. Now blessed with a title, desperate women flung themselves at him. But he wanted something more. Something deeper. Someone like…her.

"I am waiting for a man who I cannot say no to. A man whose presence in my life makes me forget I was ever a chaperone." Charlotte did not know where the words were coming from. Perhaps a deep place within her, somewhere she had placed her hopes and dreams years ago when she had said goodbye to them forever. "A man who will make me feel like a bride for the rest of my life."

William stopped dead in his tracks.

She knew it was too much to ask of anyone and should not have been too open. "What are you…oh!"

It had been impossible to continue talking as the heavens opened. Torrential rain poured down, and Charlotte laughed with the suddenness of it all.

"Goodness!" Her bonnet started to droop under the watery on-slaught, and William laughed.

"Come on, the Pump Room is just around the corner, we can take cover there!"

He took her hand, and it felt like the most natural thing in the world. As they stepped inside the Pump Room, they wrung the water out from their sleeves.

"Ah, darling, I did not see you there!"

The voice rang out across the room as Charlotte shook herself dry.

"It looks like you have already been spotted," William's voice was wry. "Am I to share you with the whole of Bath society?"

She looked up and saw Lady Romeril. "Her ladyship is not hailing me. Can you not see Miss Worsley over there? She is back in town."

Had it been a month since they had first met? His conduct toward her had always been honorable, even when he had been seducing her. She had heard nothing bad about him from anyone in society, not really. And he had been within moments of proposing...

Charlotte shivered. "We had better circulate, and separately if we do not want the gossips of the world to talk."

"Let them talk," William said with a grin. "I care not what they say about us."

She shook her head. "You may not, but I do. I will take a turn about the room and meet you back here in twenty minutes."

Without waiting for his response, she allowed herself to join the gentle flow around the room. It was impossible to explain to him how exhilarating his intensity was. After giving up the hope of marriage, to have it suddenly thrust upon her...

It was overwhelming.

"Ah, Lady Charlotte!"

It was Miss Seton, and she was bearing down on her like a fox on the hunt, ignoring those whose paths she interrupted, her eyes firmly set on Charlotte.

"Miss Seton," Charlotte said, dropping into a curtsey.

The lady followed suit and immediately said, "Dear Lord, am I glad to have come across you here, for I did not know which rooms you had taken this Season and 'tis so difficult to find out how to send a letter without direction! And how are you, Lady Charlotte?"

Charlotte opened her mouth to respond, but Miss Seton was too hasty for her.

"I must ask you, before you are swept away by this tide of people," falling into step with her, "whether you are engaged next Thursday evening?"

Charlotte felt a slow swell of happiness. It had been weeks since any of her acquaintances had engaged her company for the evening. This was truly a good day.

"I believe I am unengaged for Thursday," she replied.

"Thank heavens!" Miss Seton's loud exclamation drew the notice of those around them. "I had been tearing my hair out, Lady Charlotte, but as soon as I saw you, I thought it would all come right, and now the table is complete!"

Charlotte smiled at Miss Seton's enthusiasm. "I presume this is a dining engagement?"

"Oh, Lord, yes. I had two baronets and Lady Romeril, of course, and the three Belcher brothers, which left me unbalanced, you see," explained Miss Seton breezily. "And with Miss Marnion being courted by the younger Belcher, I simply had to have a chaperone at the table to even the numbers and to ensure Miss Marnion's protection. Seven o'clock then, this Thursday, my rooms—I'm in Grosvenor Square. Good day, Lady Charlotte!"

Without another word, Miss Seton stepped away into the stream of people.

Charlotte's shoulders slumped. She should have guessed. *Of course, Miss Seton does not wish her to attend on her own merit. She does not want to hear Charlotte's opinion on art or music. She does not want the pleasure of seeing Charlotte dance or hear her sing.*

Her merit was as chaperone, the world's only view of her: a rather convenient spinster.

She reached the other end of the room and obediently followed the flow to turn around the room.

As Charlotte allowed the chatter of the room to wash over her, she tried to imagine being married to William—being married at all.

It was impossible. She had never been this close to marriage in her entire life, and as she had told William what felt like a lifetime ago, her only experience of marriage—her parents—was hardly a shining example.

She could have stayed at Stonehaven Lacey with Richard and Tabitha. It would certainly have been awkward at the beginning, to be sure, but after a while, they would have all become accustomed to each other, then perhaps she could have seen what a genuine marriage looks like.

A meeting of minds and hearts. A balance of opinions and passions. What it was to care for someone and be cared for in return.

Charlotte smiled despite herself. Instead, she had returned to Bath and discovered a gentleman who was ready to look past everything, her age, her reticence to be drawn into conversation with him, her innocence, and distrust.

Her wandering eyes caught sight of a tall man with sharp blue eyes.

William was walking in the opposite direction, and Charlotte's breath caught. The sight of him, tall and handsome, elegantly dressed and with so much energy, so much charisma, the dampness of the rain still apparent in his hair...

His eyes caught hers. Without looking at those whom he pushed past, he began walking straight toward her, ignoring the affronted murmurs around him.

Charlotte's heart was thumping painfully in her chest, and she stopped walking. She would jump into matrimony with him. William was the one who could make marriage not frightening but exciting. After all these years of being convinced she would be alone for the rest of her life, the two of them together have found happiness.

Without thinking, Charlotte began to walk toward William, and they met, breathless and silent, in the middle of the Pump Room.

Charlotte drank in the sight of him. She desperately wanted to say

something, but what? He was staring silently, and Charlotte desperately wanted him to speak.

As she opened her mouth, William said, "I have hated being apart
from you."

He looked nervous. It was not an emotion she had seen on his
features before, but it became him. That arrogant, self-assured look
was gone. Now there was a charming vulnerability.

"Have you?" she managed. "It has only been five minutes."

He nodded. "I have something important to say to you. To ask
you here in this public place. Where a refusal to my question would be
very embarrassing for me."

Charlotte's heart skipped a beat. Was this it? Was this the moment
when he finally proposed in the way she had described?

Seeing the fear and anticipation in his eyes, seeing he was unsure
whether she would accept.... He was just as afraid as she was. She was
apprehensive about marriage, the commitment it brought—and so
was he. Opening yourself up to another person was terrifying and he
felt it too.

She loved that about him. She loved so much about him, she was
unsteadied on her feet by the thought of it. How had she mistaken this
love, this devotion to him, for anything else?

"Lady Charlotte," he said quietly and began to bend his knee.

"Ah, Your Grace!"

William straightened so quickly, he seemed to pull a muscle in his
neck. Charlotte whirled around to see who had unwisely interrupted
what was to be the most romantic occasion of her life, and saw two
women hurrying towards them, evidently mother and daughter by the
similarity in their noses.

"I thought it was you!" The mother said accusingly to William.
"Mrs. Holmes. We were introduced at the Winter Ball in London."

Could she not see she had interrupted a private conversation? The
daughter certainly seemed to recognize her impropriety and tugged at

her mother's sleeve to pull her away.

"Now then, Mary, His Grace will not mind," soothed her mother, who immediately turned to William before he could speak. "I did think it was you there, Your Grace, and I was surprised, for I did not think you would come to the Pump Room, and here you are. Mary, I said, we absolutely must find his Grace the Duke of Mercia, and here you are!"

Charlotte glanced at William, who evidently had no idea who the woman was and had no wish to speak with her. Charlotte almost laughed aloud at the ridiculousness of it all. Was this Mrs. Holmes to keep them from happiness with her inane chatter?

"Such a pleasure to speak with you," Mrs. Holmes was saying. "Now I heard tell from Miss Theodosia Ashbrooke, a lovely lady, I must say, that you were in the marriage market! And this is a very fine thing, for there are simply not the same caliber of eligible men I enjoyed in my youth, and Mr. Holmes was the cream of the crop. But as I was saying, you are currently seeking a bride, which is all to the good, and I wished to introduce you to my daughter, Mary, who, as you can see, is quite beautiful and not at all proud for it. I said to her the other day…"

Charlotte scrunched her nose at the awkwardness of the situation. To think, Mrs. Holmes believed it appropriate to accost poor Will in the Pump Room and offer her daughter on a silver platter!

She cast an eye at Miss Holmes, expecting to see her equally as mortified by her mother's rudeness in interrupting their conversation—and more, to be horrified that her mother was so blatantly attempting to secure Will as a son-in-law.

To her horror, the uncomfortable look had utterly disappeared from Miss Holmes, and she was smiling rather coquettishly at the handsome duke.

"—and so, I had to agree, for who am I to disagree with a viscount, especially one who considered my Mary so fine!" Mrs. Holmes drew breath, and William opened his mouth—but he missed his chance. "Although he was not the first to spot my Mary's beauty, and I am certain he will not be the last, for when we had the Lady Romeril for dinner—you must know the Lady Romeril, everyone does. Why, even she said…"

Disgust overwhelmed Charlotte, and not at Mrs. Holmes, but the entire marriage market. It was worse than a cattle market, with the best beauties paraded to see how much men would bid for them. To think she had ever been a part of it, chaperoning women to ensure they hooked their gentleman. It was barbaric!

But her thoughts were interrupted as she was directly addressed by Mrs. Holmes.

"I am sure the Lady Charlotte will agree to be your chaperone, will you not, Lady Charlotte?" Mrs. Holmes beamed at her, and then turned to her daughter and spoke in a mock whisper, "I know the Lady Charlotte will oblige, my dear, for she is not one to begrudge the young and beautiful, though she has not enjoyed the fruits of matrimony herself."

For the first time in her life, Charlotte felt the rage of her father erupt and did absolutely nothing to stop it.

"How dare you!" she exploded, her voice carrying. "How dare you speak to me in such a way—nay, *about* me in such a way! Your disrespectful attitude is disgraceful, and I am ashamed to hear it, let alone be its subject!"

Mrs. Holmes was staring, aghast, along with most of the Pump Room. Charlotte did not care. She was already stared at for being a spinster, laughed at for being a chaperone, but it was time to be gossiped about something she had actually done.

"For once in my life, I am not going to fade into the background of other people's lives," she stormed, advancing on the helpless Mrs. Holmes with a finger raised. Will took her hand and hastily held onto it, but Charlotte did not look at him. "I am tired of being the punchline to jokes! For once, you are going to look at me and see a woman, not just a handy chaperone who can act as part of the furniture to marry off your daughter!"

Charlotte's heavy breathing was the only sound. Everyone stood transfixed, staring.

"Lady Charlotte!" Mrs. Holmes breathed. "I did not mean…I did not intend…"

"Charlotte, marry me." Will's voice echoed in the silent room. He stepped close to her and whispered in her ear so no one else could hear him. "My heart cannot continue on like this. Marry me, or I will leave Bath. I am tired of you acting as a chaperone to half the women in the county when you are the most beautiful and most spirited one among them."

Charlotte turned to look into his eyes but could not speak. Excitement was pumping through her veins, and she wanted to hurt someone, or be held by him, or run away and never see any of them ever again, and she did not know which.

"You love me. Did you not say so?"

Her cheeks colored at asking such a question before such a crowd, but before he could reply, Miss Holmes spoke into the silence.

"Your Grace, are you in love with this chaperone?" Miss Holmes looked between them in astonishment. "Is…is that allowed?"

Charlotte's gray eyes turned to Will. He tipped back his head and laughed. He did not defend her or protect her. He stood there, chuckling in the silence, ignoring the crowd watching her as though she was the entertainment for the day.

The pain in her heart peaked. Was she a joke to him? Had he no feelings at all? The love he was about to profess could not be real. If he cared for her at all, he would never allow her to be mocked like this in public.

"What do you have to say to that?" she whispered, not taking her eyes from him.

Will stopped laughing, and his eyes flickered from Mrs. Holmes to Miss Holmes to her.

Attempting to hold back tears and knowing she could not do so for long, Charlotte laughed bitterly. "And to think that I was about to accept—this, I think, is the perfect example of why I cannot be your wife."

"No—no Charlotte, you have misunderstood me," Will said, but he was still smiling, and it cut into her soul.

"I do not have to listen to this," said Charlotte, taking a step away from him toward the door, toward freedom. "I do not have to listen to you. Good day, Your Grace."

The tears then fell, and she let them fall as she walked in silence through the staring Pump Room. They fell the entire time it took her to reach home, and they did not cease falling until many hours later.

CHAPTER SIXTEEN

T HE GLASS SLAMMED onto the table, dregs of ale sloshing over the lip.

"...and that," William said impressively, "is what happened."

His words were met with silence by the other four gentlemen around the table in the York Club. John was seated beside him and was staring into his glass, as though unsure how it had emptied so fast. The other three were shaking their heads, and William felt a surge of irritation. Did they not understand? Had they not heard how ridiculous it was?

"And did you follow her?" Charles Audley, Duke of Orrinshire, sipped at his ale with an eyebrow raised.

William shrugged. "What was the point? Charlotte had made herself perfectly clear. She does not wish to marry me, and that's an end to it. I leave Bath tomorrow."

There was silence around the table, though there was raucous laughter from the rest of the room. The night was late, and the ale was flowing, feeding the merriment in the place.

But not with William and his companions. The day's events blurred through drink and irritation, but they still stung.

Pain rocketed through his body as John punched him in the arm.

"God's teeth, that hurt!" William rubbed at the place where his brother's fist had fallen. "What was that for?"

"You absolute fool," John said with no sympathy whatsoever.

William was incensed to see their three friends, Orrinshire, Lord George Northmere, and Josiah Stanhope, Earl of Chester, were nodding in agreement. "Fool? I fail to see what I could have done differently, you blaggard, and you were not even there!"

"Not laughing would have been a good place to start," said Lord George as he drained his glass and placed it on the table beside William's. He gestured at one of the serving girls shepherded by a footman in the Club's livery, who nodded and disappeared to find a pitcher.

William could not help but feel a twinge of shame. "I admit, it was not one of my finest moments—but Christ, it was all so ridiculous! Mrs. Holmes standing there, all agog at being shouted at, Miss Holmes thrusting her bosom at me like a wanton, and I could not have been less interested in the poor thing."

Chester snorted. "Not really the point, though, is it, Mercia?"

"I have never seen Charlotte as a chaperone," William persisted, "and it makes me laugh that everyone else does. 'Tis not a crime to see the funny side!"

The serving girl approached their table with a pitcher filled to the brim with a local ale and left it on the table. Chester watched her go appreciatively, and when Lord George kicked him under the table, he raised his hands in mock surrender.

"Look," Chester said in a tone of finality, refilling his tankard, "if you had half a brain, you would have known how Charlotte would react. How any woman would have taken it! God's teeth man, you have a sister, you know what women are like."

"Two sisters," John corrected, but with no malice in his voice. He stretched and settled again on the stool, the only one of the five not in proper seats.

William glanced at him, but his brother said nothing more. Two sisters, yes, if God was good.

Lord George was nodding. "I am married, my boys, and so I can tell you for certain, Mercia. Women do not like to be laughed at. Especially not in public."

"You learned that the hard way!" Orrinshire guffawed, and he was joined in his merriment by everyone at the table, except William.

He bit his lip. Now he looked back on it, laughter was probably not the cleverest reaction—it had all seemed like a play put on for his own amusement. That anyone would look at Charlotte, brilliant and beautiful, and see an accessory to courtship! He poured himself another drink from the rapidly emptying pitcher.

"The real question is," John said after his laughter had died away, "is how long has she been keeping you on this leash?"

William frowned. "What do you mean?"

"Well, when was it you first proposed?"

Shifting uncomfortably in his seat, William hesitated before responding and finally said, "I am not...exactly sure."

Lord George's jaw dropped, and his drink slopped onto the floor.

"Damn it, man, if you are not sure, how can you expect Charlotte to know?" Chester shook his head with a sad smile.

William tried to ignore the table beside them, evidently attempting to listen to their conversation. "Do not misunderstand me," he said hastily, "it is...well, I have mentioned marriage so often, it is hard to say exactly when the first time was, you see?"

This explanation did not remove his friends' concerns; if anything, it increased them.

"Mentioning marriage," said Lord George heavily, "is not the same as offering it. Blast it all, Mercia, you're not a fledgling of eighteen!"

"It was the heat of the moment!" William protested, gulping another mouthful of ale as though that would help him defend himself. "And in that heat of the moment, 'tis a challenge to get your words straight!"

Both Orrinshire and Chester grinned, the latter raising a suggestive eyebrow.

William glared at them sternly. "It is not like that. Christ, sometimes I feel like I *am* a fledgling of eighteen when I am with her. I get...God's teeth, I cannot believe I am saying this but...flustered? 'Tis the only word I can think of. My heart races, I feel hot, and my brain seems to seep out of my ears..."

His voice trailed off, and his gaze dropped to his tankard. He felt weak, out of his depth. Like he could be felled by a feather in the breeze. No man could endure it. No man should.

When he finally got the courage to lift his head, he saw his friends were looking at him seriously, without mockery.

Lord George was nodded. "That is exactly how you feel when you meet her, Mercia. 'Tis how I felt when I met and married my wife. But that's the difference, you idiot. I knew that, I told her, I proposed, and I got married."

"You were a fool not to do it properly," Orrinshire said quietly.

William hated that they were right. How had he managed to get into this position? Getting into her bedchamber was far easier than getting into her heart.

To give his hands something to do, he took a long draught from the tankard. It did not help. Now his head hurt, but it was nothing to the hurt residing in his chest.

How could he have laughed? He was so stupid! She had needed him, and he had been given the chance to show her how he cared for her. But he had not been able to help himself. He wished to God he had been able to. Would he be with her, seated in her home, discussing their wedding, where they were to live, how many children they would have?

His stomach tightened. Instead, he was here, in the York Club, sitting with his brother and friends, realizing what a fool he was.

"I have talked of marriage half a dozen times since we first met," he said quietly, more to his tankard than to anyone in particular, "and each time she has declined."

"Do you know why?"

Orrinshire's question resounded in his mind before William answered.

"She says," he explained heavily, "she is just a chaperone. She does not expect to get married, she does not trust my intentions, and she cannot imagine herself getting married. Each excuse is a variation on a theme. She is always the chaperone and never the bride."

There was more silence after this pronouncement, and then John spoke with a grin.

"Well," he said matter-of-factly, "I can understand why she thinks that. I mean, she must be what—over thirty? Five and thirty, I heard. That is old, Mercia, too old for marriage."

William did not think. His fist moved around fast and punched John firmly in the face.

John fell backward off his stool with a cry of pain, his hands clutching his face. Blood poured through his fingers.

William had risen from his chair, which had tipped over but was prevented from advancing on his brother because Orrinshire and Lord George were holding him back. He had not even noticed them move.

The club was silent, all heads turned to the fallen man on the ground. A pair of footmen moved slowly forward to check on the fallen man, and one proffered a handkerchief. Some in the room continued to stare, but the York had seen its fair share of disagreements, and this was between brothers. The murmurings rose, and the noisy chatter returned.

Chester had rushed to John's side. "Christ, John, are you hurt? Is it broken?"

John accepted his hand. Standing unsteadily, he stared at his brother.

William stared back. He was panting, his heart thudding against his ribcage. He had never done anything so violent away from the battlefield and hated the taste of anger on his tongue—but had been so overcome with the desire to protect Charlotte, her name, and her honor.

"Take that back." He was amazed he was able to speak, there was so little breath in his lungs, but the words managed to make their way out.

John's nose was bleeding badly, but he did nothing to prevent the flow, allowing it to drip down his face, onto his collar and cravat. He stared at his elder brother without saying a word.

"I apologize. Hell's bells, William, you know I like Charlotte. I was…it was wrong. I am sorry."

Remorse burned through William. He reached out a hand, and his brother took it. "It is nothing."

Orrinshire picked up the fallen stool and chair, and all five sat in silence.

John pulled out a handkerchief and started dabbing at the ebbing flow of his nose. "If Charlotte is that important," he said thickly, "why are you here talking to us, instead of out there talking to her?"

He shrugged. That was a question he could not answer.

John snorted. "It sounds like she is afraid. If the five of us have learned anything, it's that you are most afraid when you have the most to lose."

CHAPTER SEVENTEEN

C HARLOTTE PAUSED BEFORE the door and took a deep breath. No matter what, she was going to keep calm. She was not going to lose her temper again. Not like the Pump Room.

She stepped into the dimly lit breakfast room. There were two candles in the room, and Matthews was still laying the table.

"You have risen early, my..." Matthews broke off as he lifted his head.

Charlotte flushed. She had glanced quickly at her appearance in the looking glass and seen the red-ringed eyes, the disheveled hair, the hastily tied gown hanging strangely because she had not waited for Danvers to help her. She still clutched a blanket around her shoulders.

Matthews decided not to say anything and returned to his task.

Charlotte did not have the words to thank him. Instead, she sat at the table, sinking into the cushioned seat. The morning had come too quickly, and she still could not believe yesterday had even happened.

"Your Grace, are you in love with this chaperone? Is...is that allowed?"

"I hope you enjoy today's breakfast," Matthews said quietly, jolting Charlotte back to the present. "I have been informed that Cook has saved some delicious kippers, especially for today. The evening post was delivered late, and I have placed the letters here."

He gestured towards the pile of letters before her plate, and Charlotte nodded.

"Tea has been poured, and as usual, ring the bell if you need anything."

Charlotte found her voice was hoarse when she spoke. "Thank you, Matthews."

Matthews paused by her chair, but then nodded and left the room without speaking.

Sighing, Charlotte leaned back in her chair and listened. The only sound was the ticking of the clock. For the first time since his marriage, she missed Richard. She never thought she would miss him at breakfast, of all times in the day, but no matter what wild time of night he returned from one of his parties, or balls, or card tables, he would always make the effort to drag himself up and have breakfast with her.

Now she breakfasted alone.

The clock ticked away the minutes, and Charlotte realized she had not moved. Leaning forward to help herself to tea, she raised the cup to her lips, took a refreshing sip, and looked at the letters waiting for her.

She had hoped at least one of the six letters would be from Richard or Tabitha, but as she perused them, none of the handwriting seemed familiar.

Matthews had thoughtfully left the letter opener beside her plate, and after taking a gulp of tea to soothe her throat, sore from crying, Charlotte slit open the first letter.

It was not long, and as she perused the lines, a frown appeared between her eyes. Putting it aside and taking a long deep breath, she opened another. It was almost identical to the first.

Five of the letters were opened, read carefully, and laid in a row across her plate. She drank the last of the tea in her cup and read the longest again.

Dear Lady Charlotte,

I do hope you are not alarmed by receiving a letter from me as I know we are not intimate, but I wanted to communicate my thanks to you and could think of no better way than this.

I am truly grateful that you chaperoned me with William Lennox, Duke of Mercia, especially your fortuitous seating arrangement at the opera. I am even more grateful for the park excursion for it gave John, the Marquess of Gloucester, I mean—and I the opportunity to speak openly, and my heart is more full of him than I can say.

There have been some rumors, I have just been informed, that I have been accepting the addresses of Philip Egerton, Earl of Marnmouth, which could not be further from the truth. He is a great friend of my father's cousin, and so has called here several times to pay his respects. I have attempted to explain this to many people, but no one believes me, and all I can do is think of John.

If I am honest, I believe he loves me almost as much as I adore him, but with the spring here, many people are returning to the country, and I am in need of at least one more opportunity to fix him. I am sure that, with encouragement, he will make me the happiest person on this earth and ask me to be

But no. I cannot even write it, in case all my hopes are for naught. Please, Lady Charlotte, will you do me the honor of acting as our chaperone again? It would mean the world to me and could make all the difference.

I know you are a chaperone for many ladies, but if you could find room for me, my father and I will be eternally in your debt.

I am your ever-affectionate friend,
Miss Rebecca Darby

Charlotte leaned back in her chair. Each of the letters were written in the same vein. I should not be writing to you, Lady Charlotte, but I am; I want to be married, Lady Charlotte, and to this gentleman in particular; please, Lady Charlotte, be our chaperone.

This was her life. Watching from a seat, not part of the dance itself but merely an admirer of those who took the steps. Watching everyone else find their happily ever after. She was truly the chaperone in every social occasion, never to be the bride at all.

"You have never been a chaperone to me, but a captivating lady."

Charlotte shivered, despite the warmth of the blanket still tight around her shoulders. Will wanted to marry her. He saw past the label of chaperone and saw her. It had been difficult to believe him, and for a while, she could not have imagined herself as a lady courted by such a man. *Any man.*

But then that night when she had invited him to her bedchamber...

She shivered, but this time due to the remembrance of desire. She had never known a man to be so persistent. Even some of those she has chaperoned had not been this determined!

She poured more tea and added a wedge of lemon, which was Cook's latest indulgence. It was not enough that he haunted her every waking step, but she was dreaming about him, too, and even when awake, she could think of no one but Will.

By God, she loved him. It had twisted her heart, his laughter the day before, when she had felt her most vulnerable when she had been mocked by society for the most excruciating...

The memory of Mrs. Holmes's flabbergasted face popped into her mind, and Charlotte snorted with laughter—and put her hands over her mouth in horror. Now that she thought more about it, it seemed ridiculous. The simpering daughter, the overly eager mother, herself and Will stuck in the middle, attempting to have their own moment of love.

Remorse filled her heart. He had laughed, and perhaps out of nerves as well as the stupidity of the scene. Just as she realized how much she loved him and how precious he was, he had laughed, and she stormed out of the Pump Room.

Would he ever propose to her again? Would he even want to see her again? Wild panic flooded through Charlotte as she tried to see the whole situation as an outsider. If she was Will, would she want to propose again?

Her heart plummeted to her feet, bypassing her stomach. Certainly not. Had he not attempted to persuade her? Had he not made love to her, kissed her, and been honest with her?

Charlotte glanced at the fifth letter, the one from Miss Darby, and read it again.

> *There have been some rumors, I have just been informed...which could not be further from the truth, but no one believes me, and all I can do is think of John.*
>
> *If I am honest, I believe he loves me almost as much as I adore him. I am in need of at least one more opportunity...he will make me the happiest person on this earth and ask me to be...*
>
> *But no. I cannot even write it, in case all my hopes are for naught.*

Miss Darby. Foolish, chattering, Miss Darby. Charlotte had been so dismissive of her, and her words rang true in her heart, as though her mother was beside her, guiding Miss Darby's pen to give her exactly the advice she needed.

One more opportunity to fix him. He will make me the happiest person on this earth and ask me to be... But no. I cannot even write it, in case all my hopes are for naught.

Charlotte tightened her grip on the letter. How different were she and Miss Darby? They had both been expecting something different when they had met a gentleman who made them feel...everything. Everything was different, everything new.

Their happiness depended on that gentleman, but they were both one proposal away from true happiness. If they were both to gain their hearts' desires, they would become sisters, which a strange thought.

Charlotte started as the most wild and reckless idea came to her mind. Being a chaperone had started as a favor to a friend, and where had it led? To becoming what society had expected of her: a dull, cowed, and quiet chaperone.

But she was Lady Charlotte St. Maur. She was the daughter of a duke, and what's more, she possessed intelligence and common sense. She had a man who loved her.

One letter was still lying unopened on the table. The handwriting looked strangely familiar, and when she opened it, she smiled. It was from Tabitha.

Dearest Charlotte,

Well, the baby has shifted for the first time, and I cannot tell you how much joy it brings me! Your brother, fool that he is, is attempting to force me into bedrest when I am but four months along, but I quickly put a stop to that. My mother did not take to her bed until confinement itself, and I see no reason to be any different.

I am still discovering Stonehaven. There appear to be more doors and rooms than I had remembered each time I walk down a corridor, and I never know where I have left anything. There are approximately six half-embroidered cushions all around the place, and I haven't stumbled across the same one twice.

By the way, please thank Matthews for his continuing instructions. I am endeavoring to keep to them, but you must tell him my taste in brandy, at the very least, is not going to be tested. I will simply obey.

Richard has been wondering about names for this little one. I think he is a boy, but Richard is convinced she is a girl. Would we be asking too much if we begged your approval to call our first daughter, Charlotte? You must tell me if you would rather we did not.

Charlotte, I wish to know you better. You must come back to Stonehaven Lacey as soon as the Season is over. If you are anything like your brother, and he has assured me you are, then I feel we will become close friends.

He frightens me sometimes, your brother. To think that we almost lost each other due to jealousy, confusion, and misunderstandings. I fought for him, Charlotte, as I have never fought for anything. I thank God I did.

Do you know where the silver spoons are? I've been told Mrs. Marsh needs them and cannot find them. I must go. Please write back and tell me when you'll be back.

I remain ever your sister,
Tabitha, Duchess of Axwick

Charlotte swallowed. Her fingers brushed the ink on the page. How could Tabitha know just how timely her letter was?

I fought for him, Charlotte, as I have never fought for anything.

She had seen the true affection between her brother and his new wife and never thought to experience the same. But without seeking it, without realizing it was coming, she had almost stumbled across something just as beautiful.

William Lennox, Duke of Mercia. He had been true to her, sought her out, never lied to her, or taken advantage of her. He made her heart sing.

Without any warning, Charlotte rose from her seat, allowing the blanket to fall to the floor. All this time, she had lived by society's rules, and had it made her happy?

No.

And so, what better way to win him than to court William as he had courted her? To ignore society's rules, of course. But with Will at stake, after rebutting him so definitely and then realizing how she truly felt, how he truly felt.

It was time for something drastic. Something wild. Something she would have never considered in her wildest dreams even a year ago. If she wanted to leave her chaperoning days behind her and become, truly, the bride, it would need to be something daring.

An image sparked across her imagination. It was wild. It was reckless. It was the sort of thing she could never have countenanced even a week ago. It was daring. No one would forget it. But would it be enough?

It surely wouldn't work, would it?

CHAPTER EIGHTEEN

I T WAS IMPOSSIBLE. No matter how hard he tried, William was unable to prevent himself from yawning.

"The hem itself is…Your Grace. Your Grace, I am not boring you, am I?"

Innocent eyes stared at him from the woman who had been lecturing him on the infinite number of materials used to construct her gown. Her mother stood a few paces behind her, a respectable distance to ensure nothing untoward occurred.

William sighed. It was not her fault, of course. These girls, they were taught nothing of use. Sewing and crocheting and embroidery, dancing and music, horse riding if they were lucky, and long, heartening walks in the rain if they were not…

It all led to an accomplished lady, he was sure, but interesting?

No. Miss Coulson had been introduced to him the moment he had entered Lady Romeril's second ball of the Season, and he had been unable to rid himself of her or her mother for the last hour. Chester had been throwing him envious glances, and he wished he could palm her off on him.

But no, Miss Coulson evidently wanted to be the future Duchess of Mercia, and so William was trapped by the wall near the card room, unable to free himself to play a hand or join the dancers.

Instead, he was being rewarded—if you could use that term—for his gentility with Miss Coulson by being distracted from thoughts of

Charlotte.

Goddamnit. Now he was thinking about Charlotte.

"No, I assure you," he said to Miss Coulson, whose shoulders immediately relaxed. "I never realized before how much skill and artistry goes into creating such a masterpiece as that gown. Please, do go on."

She beamed. "Well, you are in luck, Your Grace, for we have come to perhaps, nay, certainly the most interesting part. As I was saying, the hem…"

William scratched his nose in an attempt to hide his next yawn, for it was impossible to stifle. Ye gods, he should never have come. All he wanted was to ignore the world for allowing him to have fallen in love with Charlotte when he did not deserve her.

John was right: he was a fool.

Now he was paying the price for his stupidity, stuck with one of the most boring debutantes who had entered society, and it served him right.

The dancers flew past them in a speedy English country dance, and Miss Coulson took a brief look at them before continuing, "I know what you are going to say. They could not possibly have stitched each individually, but if you look here…"

William bowed his head to examine the sleeve. This will teach him not to be so easily flattered. He had heard Lady Romeril hosted but one ball a Season, which had been a few months ago. When the invitation for a second ball had arrived, it was considered unprecedented, and no one had managed to pry the reason from Lady Romeril's lips.

Even Mrs. Bryant, the renowned gossip of Bath was none the wiser—and this had whipped the intrigue into a frenzy. By the time it had come to respond to the invitation, William had allowed his curiosity to get the better of him.

Trust him to be introduced to the most boring woman in the room. The trouble was, he had stood for so long and feigned interest so well, he was not entirely sure how to extricate himself from her tiresome company. If matters did not resolve themselves, and quickly, he could find himself trapped with Miss Coulson for the remainder of the evening.

"But the hair, the hair is something else quite entirely," said Miss Coulson, raising an elegant hand to gesture towards the pile of curls entangled with pearls. "You see, while you may think you need to begin with the curling irons, you must instead..."

William's eyes slid from the piled hair upon Miss Coulson's head to the lady walking leisurely past them. Dark hair, bedroom eyes, and a lingering look.

Miss Emma Tilbury, famed companion to the Earl of Marnmouth, winked as she passed him and cast an amused eye at Miss Coulson.

William smiled, despite himself, and waved her away. So, he was not the only one who had noticed Miss Coulson's rather unfortunate interest in dressmaking. He should have known Miss Tilbury would do something as wild as winking at him in a ball—but then, if Marnmouth was to believed, there was little Miss Tilbury would not do.

Unfortunately, the interaction between him and Miss Tilbury had been noticed by a trio of ladies who had returned with glasses of punch.

William froze. *Oh, Christ. Don't tell me they're all going to be at it.*

But his fears were confirmed when the other two ladies walked past him as Miss Coulson chattered on, winking mischievously.

The marriage market was hell on earth. How did anyone manage to navigate it—and why did they bother? It was full of traps and snares for the innocent, and many women entered it without any of the right tools. Take poor, Miss Coulson. Unless she was able to find a tailor, she might end her days as a chaperone.

His stomach tightened. Even he had slipped into that horrendous way of thinking. No wonder Charlotte hated being a chaperone so fiercely; there was no better way for a woman to be considered useless and unmarriageable than to describe her as a chaperone or spinster, and even he had fallen into that habit.

Charlotte. Even thinking her name was painful, but he knew she was lost to him. There was no chance in hell she would even consider him as a dance partner now, let alone a partner for life. In all honesty, he could not blame her.

"For once in my life, I am not going to fade into the background of other people's lives!"

"…and with careful study, one is able to apply the pearls in a circular motion, like so, to prevent them dropping in the heat of a ball. Of course, if diamonds are your preferred choice…"

William let Miss Coulson's words wash over him. There was nothing in Bath for him, not after burning his bridges so definitely with Charlotte. He would wait out the ball, try and find out why Lady Romeril had decided to go against her convention and host a second of the Season, then leave for home.

At least then, he could not drive himself mad by hoping to see Charlotte every time he turned a corner, or entered a shop, or walked into a room. Christ, it was as bad as Honora, wherever she was. His whole life, every breath seemed to be on hold for these two women. He would die for them, each of them, but he was no closer either than he was three years ago.

A gaggle of newcomers entered the room, and William's heart skipped a beat when he saw a dull gray gown, but then it sank. It was not Charlotte.

In a strange way, he was glad. He did not want to see Charlotte again here, in a private ball full of strangers. What would he do when he next saw her? Mouth dry up, heart stop, stomach lurch?

Or perhaps, and the thought was physical pain across his forehead, he would not see her again. She did not appear to be at Lady Romeril's ball, and if he carried out his plan and left in the morning, there was little chance of a meeting again.

"Ahem." Miss Coulson was staring, obviously awaiting a response.

William hoped he was charming. "I do apologize, Miss Coulson, I thought I saw...an acquaintance enter the room. Would you be so good as to repeat that?"

A true smile crept over Miss Coulson's face. "Of–of course, Your Grace! Well, as I said at the beginning, this gown is silk, of course, but 'tis not the silk one would normally find in..."

William groaned inwardly.

What he would do for Charlotte's company.

He should have proposed properly, securing her hand from the moment he knew he could not live without her.

"You can barely notice unless you examine it carefully. And that is all to the good, if you ask me."

He could have immediately explained who Prudence was. Teasing was all very well, but it had overwrought Charlotte's emotions. He should never have done that.

"But of course, my favorite part, as I said before, is the sleeves. See how the stitching, so small and so careful, never going beyond the lines of the design."

The more he looked back, the more mistakes he recognized. No wonder she had eventually walked away. She deserved better, more than a thoughtless laugh when she had needed him. That laugh had broken everything between them, and he would never get the chance to make it right.

"Do you agree?"

William started. "What?"

For the first time since they had been introduced, Miss Coulson scowled. "I...I do not think you have been listening to a word I have said, Your Grace."

"Of course I have!" William said bracingly. "Please do continue, Miss Coulson, I was greatly enjoying hearing about the...erm...the stitching of the sleeves and the...the embroidery of the–the hem?"

Without saying another word but giving him a dirty look, Miss

Coulson bobbed her head and stalked back to her mother.

Finally. William breathed out slowly and leaned against the wall, finally alone with his thoughts.

He pulled out his pocket watch. Already a quarter to ten. All he had to do was survive for another few hours. At Lady Romeril's balls it was considered good manners to leave as soon as she had gone to bed, and that was never late. A couple of hours and he could leave, and then depart Bath in the morning. There was nothing left for him here.

Confused murmurings rose from the dancers, and William glanced over curiously.

People started to point. Was this some special entertainment Lady Romeril had organized? Was she to make an announcement, perhaps?

The hostess did enjoy drama.

The dancers started to move aside. A woman dressed in the most exquisite gown and drenched in diamonds, and wearing a tiara—the sort a duchess would wear.

She had such presence. William could feel it from the other side of the room. No wonder the dancers were moving aside for her—carriages on the street would move aside for her.

William's jaw dropped. *It was Charlotte.*

But not the Charlotte ignored by the world. This one was adorned with diamonds—her neck, her wrists, her ears. The gown was shapely but modest, hinting at the splendid figure William knew all too well was under that silk.

It wasn't what she was wearing that was astonishing, but the way she moved, no longer apologetic or quiet, or hoping not to be noticed. This was a woman confident and graceful woman, unafraid of everything.

It was a true marvel to see her flaunting her beauty.

Heart thundering, he went to her, humbled and eager to hear her voice, to be the recipient of her glorious smile. "Charlotte."

The single word came out strangled, but it was all he could muster. He could see Lady Romeril grinning behind Charlotte, at the front of the crowd of spectators.

Well, he had to hand it to her, Lady Romeril had done it again. Her ball was going to be the talk of the town—but how was Charlotte involved? Was she waiting for him to say something—was this his chance to apologize?

"Charlotte—Lady Charlotte," he corrected himself. God's teeth, why was he so nervous?

But Charlotte did not appear to be listening to him. The nervousness was still dancing around her eyes. She lowered herself into an elegant curtsey, then…

William gasped, and he was not alone. Shock echoed around the room as all of Bath's elegant society watched Lady Charlotte St. Maur kneel before him.

Surely, she was not going to…was she?

"Your Grace, William," she said. The room immediately fell silent. "My whole life, I have been controlled by fear. Fear of my father. Fear of being rejected by my peers."

Her gray eyes did not waver, but he heard the quiver of pain in her voice and wanted to stop her there, pull her into his arms, and comfort her—but wild horses would not make him do it. This was what she wanted. This was her time.

"I am always a chaperone, and never the bride," she said. "Gentlemen requested my company because I gave them the chance to court beautiful women."

"I do not believe there is anyone more beautiful than…" began William, but Charlotte gave him a sharp look, and he immediately stopped.

"Then I met you," Charlotte said simply. "You saw me for me. Sought to spend time with me because you actually like me—care for me."

Yes, he did, and so much more. He reached for her, hungry for her warmth and passion. Desperate to connect with her, to marry her. "I love you," he said so everyone could hear him.

The crowd gasped, and Charlotte and William smiled at each other. Their devotion for each other undeniable.

"I love you," Charlotte said. "Though it has taken me far too long to realize it, I know we can make each other happy. If you will marry me."

William had watched her lips move, but it was hard to believe what she had said. Had Charlotte really *proposed?*

She was watching him anxiously. "Marry me?" she whispered.

Some were shaking their heads, others looked scandalized, and William saw Mrs. Bryant fan herself rapidly.

She truly loved him.

William took a step forward.

"I have been in Bath a few months, and in that time, I have met over a hundred young ladies," he said. Charlotte was still kneeling on the floor, looking up with anticipation. "Of all the women I have met, none have compared to you. Charlotte, you are the most beautiful, intelligent, and witty one of them all. Of course I will marry you."

He was ready for the world to know what he thought of her.

"I am tired," he said softly, "of seeing you relegated by society to the role of chaperone. You were always meant to be my bride. Perhaps even the mother to my children, if God is good to us. I want you, Charlotte, today and forever."

In a swift movement, he closed the distance between them, took her by the hand, and pulled her into his arms for a passionate kiss.

The world could collapse all around them, and William would not have cared. His soul was overwhelmed by Charlotte.

He wanted to lose himself in her forever.

He broke the kiss and looked into her eyes. "You proposed to me."

"I even told you how it should be done. To ask someone in a public place, where a refusal to the question would be very embarrassing."

She laughed shakily. "It made sense for me to show you after I realized how much I loved you, and that fear kept me from accepting you before."

"I love you so much." William tightened his grip on her. "And we are to be married! I have no idea how to celebrate. I can barely think."

Charlotte smiled, and it was a different smile than before. Leaning up to his ear, she whispered, "I do."

CHAPTER NINETEEN

CHARLOTTE CLUNG TO Will's hand, knowing she would never have to let go again. His fingers felt strong around hers, comforting, with the promise of something more.

"How much further?" Will sounded impatient, and she laughed as they turned a corner. The night was dark but not cold. They had anticipation to keep them warm.

"Not far," she said. "I thought you knew where my rooms were? You have been there before!"

He stopped abruptly, pulling Charlotte into his arms and kissing her deeply.

Fire existed between them, hot and wild. They controlled their feelings while still at the ball, but once they had left... It was a long way back to Number Fourteen, Queen Square.

Will tilted her head back to deepen the kiss, and Charlotte moaned at the intensity.

"I want you, Charlotte."

"Not here," she said breathlessly. "We have the rest of our lives to..."

"I have waited my whole life for you," growled Will with a wicked smile. "I cannot wait much longer."

Charlotte hesitated, then pulled his hands away and took a step back. "You will have to. Chaperone's discretion."

Will groaned. "Fine, you temptress, but you promised me it was not far."

She laughed as she led him down the street by the hand. After so many years of being alone, ignored, and unwanted, she had finally found love and happiness. After so much confusion between herself and Will, they were to marry—and she had plenty of ideas of what to do in the meantime.

Charlotte had not exaggerated. They were about five minutes away from her rooms, but that was evidently too much for Will. After turning another corner and seeing it was not her street, he groaned.

"No, this is too much," he said, and without warning, pushed her against a wall, thrusting himself against her and pouring kisses down her neck.

"Will!" She did not know whether she meant it as a halt or encouragement. All she knew was every place his lips touched burned like a brand.

"Charlotte," moaned Will, his fingers playing with the ribbons on her gown.

"Will—no!"

He chuckled as one of the ribbons holding her bodice together came undone. She twisted away, reveling in the feeling and knowledge he wanted her so badly.

His eyes were on her, and she laughed.

"You are fortunate, Your Grace, that there is no one out on the street, or my reputation would be ruined!"

"Good. That is exactly how it should be." Will moved closer. "Christ, Charlotte, if we don't hurry, then I am going to have you against this wall."

The thought of it made her shiver with pleasure, but she was not going to be tempted by such wildness. No, she was going to make him wait, and it would all be worth it.

"Down here," she said breathlessly, walking hurriedly. "Here."

They made it to her home, and she nearly tripped up the stairs to the front door.

Once inside, he reached for her. "At last, I can touch you."

His hands moved slowly and purposefully down her waist to her hips. He caressed her gently, his eyes filled with desire.

"Yes," she murmured as he trailed kisses along her neck.

As his hands moved to her breasts, she sucked in a breath, consumed by heat and need.

"God, Charlotte, you want me," he moaned in her ear. "You want me badly."

"Yes."

But as his fingers started a gentle rhythm, he stepped back.

Will was standing in the hallway, looking around nervously. She leaned against the door, staring at her future husband. Hers alone.

"What is wrong?" she asked.

"What about the servants?"

Charlotte smiled. Not answering immediately, she removed the tiara, throwing it to the floor. "What servants?"

He grinned. "Come now, Charlotte, you know who I mean. Matthews, the others. Where are they?"

She shrugged. "I gave them the night off."

Will's wandering eyes moved quickly back to her. "All of them?"

"All of them."

He took a step toward her. "The whole night?"

Charlotte licked her lips. "And tomorrow."

With a growl, he took her in his arms. "Good."

His quick fingers made light work of the few ribbons and pins keeping her gown up. They both scrambled to remove each other's clothes—the mutual desperation growing.

She belonged to him more than she belonged to herself.

After removing her shoes, Charlotte straightened up, completely naked but for the diamonds.

"I will need help," Charlotte whispered, taking in his superior form, his manhood erect and glorious. "Taking the rest of the diamonds off, I mean."

"No. Let's keep them on."

They moved at the same instant. Their lips met as his hands reached for her bottom, and she clung to him as though he was the one real thing in the world.

"Upstairs?" she managed to say.

She had expected him to eagerly accept her suggestion, perhaps to take her by the hand and lead her there.

But instead, he smiled wickedly. "No. Here."

Before Charlotte could refuse, William picked her up.

"What are you doing?"

He stepped over to the hearthrug and gently set her down.

Charlotte looked up at the most handsome man she had ever known. For an instant, she felt embarrassed and vulnerable. But she trusted him.

"Will," she said, reaching out a hand.

He did not need encouragement.

Will had moved to join her on the rug, but instead of kissing her lips, he pushed her legs aside and kissed her most intimate place. "Oh!"

Was it even possible to survive such pleasure? As his tongue flickered across her most sensitive skin, she squirmed against him, wanting more.

"Yes, Will, yes!" She tried to hold in her cries of pleasure.

He raised his head and grinned, his hands stroking her inner thighs gently. "I don't know why you are bothering to be so quiet, Charlotte. There is no one to hear us."

"I know," she panted through a haze of desire.

"So, next time, I want to hear you." He was serious. "I want to hear you shout out. I want to hear the pleasure I am giving you. I want you to scream my name."

"Next time?"

He nodded, then moved over her, his gaze unmoving. "Once I give you this." He thrust inside her, groaning.

She squirmed at the intrusion, but her body accepted him—wanted him—needed him more than ever. After several long moments of soul-stealing kisses, he withdrew from her, and said, "I want to see you on your knees before me, Charlotte."

Barely understanding through her haze of pleasure, she turned and kneeled on the hearthrug. It felt strange, facing away from him, and she did not like it at first.

His warm hands caressed her backside and inner thighs. "Trust me, Charlotte."

She did, so much.

He entered her slowly, and it was deeper and more intense than it had ever been before—wonderful.

The indescribable pleasure heightened as Will reached for one of her breasts, teasing her nipple between his fingers.

"Say my name," he growled as he started thrusting deeper inside her. "Say it."

She sobbed with pleasure. It was too much, all too much—who could ever have known such ecstasy was possible between two people?

"Say it!"

"Will," she whispered, almost unable to speak as he plunged deeper and deeper.

"Louder."

"William!"

It may have been mere seconds, but she climaxed, and so did he, and she could suddenly no longer support herself. She collapsed onto the floor with Will next to her.

"That…"

"I know," he growled, pulling her into his arms.

Charlotte could barely think, barely breathe. If this was married life, she was not going to tire of it ever.

"I love you," she murmured into his chest, her body still throbbing with pleasure.

"I love you," he whispered, kissing the top of her head. "My own chaperone for the rest of my life."

EPILOGUE

CHARLOTTE TOOK A last, lingering look at herself in the mirror, adjusting her diamond earbobs. She had worn them the night she and William had made love in the hallway of her home—many times. That caused her to smile. Today she would become Charlotte Lennox, the Duchess of Mercia.

To marry the man who had given her so much pleasure and made her feel like the most important woman in the world was a dream come true.

"You look beautiful."

The voice was timid, and Charlotte turned to smile at the nervous girl who had helped her into her gown. Lady Prudence Lennox smiled awkwardly.

Had it been three weeks since she had first met Prudence and been so unpardonably rude? How Charlotte regretted it, but she had the rest of her life to make it up to her.

"Thank you for helping me get ready this morning," she said.

Prudence smiled. "You are to be my sister—something I have missed."

Charlotte understood but would not allow sadness to overtake them. "I think I am ready," she said hastily. "And if I am not mistaken, I think everyone else is, too."

The sash window in her bedchamber was open, and along with a warm breeze, there came the peal of church bells.

Prudence nodded and picked up the posy of flowers and handed them to Charlotte. Bluebells and anemones picked in the garden at Stonehaven Lacey that morning. Charlotte felt the smoothness of the ribbon. She took a deep breath. This was no longer a fantasy!

As she stepped down the sweeping staircase, Matthews was standing there along with the entirety of the servants in a line, waiting to wish her well. A send-off for the daughter of the house of Axwick.

Charlotte's eyes filled with tears. They were, in a way, as much her family as Richard was.

"Congratulations," said Matthews quietly. "I know I speak for the whole household when I say we are all proud of you and pleased for you, my lady. Your Grace."

Inclining her head in silent thanks, Charlotte squeezed Matthews's hand and stepped through the front door. Sunshine poured onto her. There was not a cloud in the sky. It was a perfect day.

"There you are!" A deep voice boomed as her brother, Richard, strode forward with a top hat on his head and a scowl on his face. "I know it is tradition for the bride to be late, but Lotty…"

He stopped speaking as soon as he reached her, his eyes wide.

Charlotte felt the creep of concern tighten her shoulders. "Is there anything amiss? Do I have something in my teeth? Is my hair falling out already?"

Richard was staring as though he had never seen her before. "Lotty…you look beautiful."

Charlotte laughed and looked at the flowers in her hands. "Goodness, Axwick, you are not going to get emotional, are you?"

Richard shook his head, but his eyes were brighter than normal. "No, no, it is…Mother would have been so proud of you today. As I am."

She could have borne anything without tearing up, except that. The mention of their beloved mother stirred up many feelings. She felt her throat tighten.

"I know," she murmured, quietly, taking his arm. "She would have been proud of both of us. She *is* proud of both of us, especially you, another Axwick on the way!"

"Halfway there," he said breathlessly, clearing his throat. "But he'll be here before we get to the church at this rate. Where's that slip of a thing?"

Charlotte blinked. "Slip of a thing?"

"Ah, there she is—keep up, Pru!"

Trust her brother to be on familiar terms with her sister-in-law already. He never was one to stand on ceremony. She turned to see Prudence tripping down the steps to join them.

"My apologies, Lady Charlotte, Your Grace!"

"No need for apologies," said Richard. Charlotte beamed, he always did have such a way with people, a charm she had never learned. "The church is only next door."

As they walked around the corner, Charlotte saw the church decorated with festoons of flowers.

"Oh, beautiful!" she pulled away from Richard as she stepped toward the church, mouth open. "Axwick, did you know…"

"Wasn't me," he said hastily. "Matthews said the villagers came to ask him about it, whether we would mind, yesterday. Apparently, you are a popular person here in Stonehaven."

Charlotte stared. It must have taken them hours to pick all the flowers to transform every inch of the church walls into a bower. Her heart swelled. There was so much goodness in the world.

"Come on, there are people waiting for you in there," said Richard good-naturedly, offering his arm once again. "One of them is most eager to see you."

Yes, William, her love.

As she entered the church, Charlotte could not pretend she did not see the stares from women on both sides of the aisle. Were they truly shocked she was finally marrying?

They could not hurt her now. Charlotte smiled as she looked straight ahead. William Lennox, the Duke of Mercia, stood there in his military uniform, which made him look even taller than ever before.

When she finally reached the top of the aisle, she turned to hand her posy to Lady Prudence, who blushed at the attention and scuttled away to join Tabitha in the pew.

As the ceremony began and the vows went by in a rush, Charlotte could not stop looking at Will. Her lover. Her husband. Every time she admired him, she found something new to love.

He was hers. She was his.

"I now pronounce you man and wife!"

Charlotte jolted from her reverie to stare at the vicar who was beaming.

"May I be the first to congratulate you," he said. "The Duke and Duchess of Mercia!"

With her hand in his, Will led her down the aisle and squealed with delight as the village children met them at the door, throwing flower petals over them.

"Huzzah!" They cried as one. "Huzzah for the Duchess!"

William and Charlotte turned to each other, and she thought she saw a touch of sadness in his eyes. "What is it?" she asked.

"I wish…" he started but simply shook his head.

"Your sister?"

"I am determined we will find her one day," he said.

"Yes, we will," she promised with all her heart.

"But today," he said, kissing her tenderly, "we celebrate our love and joy."

The first guest to approach them was a friend of Will's. "I wish you both well," said Josiah Stanhope, Earl of Chester.

"Have you thought about it, Chester?"

Josiah frowned. "Marriage? God, no. I am exhausted enough with politics."

William grinned at Charlotte. "I do not believe there is anything so simple as finding the person you love and being with them."

"I would say you are right," retorted Josiah as other well-wishers started to get restless. "As long as you can find the person! I cannot tell you how tiring it is, all these ladies trying to catch an earl. I'm tired of the whole blasted game, the interfering mothers, and the trickery—the wigs! Mercia, you will not believe it when I tell you about this one girl I..."

But whatever story he wanted to tell, it would have to wait.

"Ah, Chester! I thought I saw you back there!" Miss Theodosia Ashbrooke, a formidable matchmaker, advanced on them. "You thought you could hide from me, then? Not a chance, my dear boy—no, I have just the person for you, and there is no running from me this time!"

Charlotte could not help but laugh at the haunted look on Josiah's face as he resigned himself to a conversation with Miss Ashbrooke, someone most of the landed gentry and titled nobility attempted to avoid.

But she could think no longer on Josiah, not with so many guests to greet. It was over an hour later when she noticed her husband raise an eyebrow and jerk his head over to the house.

With bows all around and a rare smile from Lady Romeril, who stood nearby, Charlotte walked arm in arm with Will back to the house.

"What?" she whispered once they were out of sight of their guests. "What was so important we had to leave?"

Her mouth was stopped by a passionate kiss. It was fortunate they were truly alone, for it would have been most unseemly for their guests to see the new Duchess of Mercia grasp at her husband in such a manner.

"Do you think we can get away with making love in *this* hallway?"

Charlotte raised an eyebrow at her husband's suggestion, scandalized but already imagining it.

"No," she said finally. "But Stonehaven Lacey has over twenty bedrooms. Choose one."

Laughing together and almost stumbling on the staircase as they rushed upstairs, Charlotte knew no one would ever mistake her for a chaperone again.

About Emily E K Murdoch

If you love falling in love, then you've come to the right place.

I am a historian and writer and have a varied career to date: from examining medieval manuscripts to designing museum exhibitions, to working as a researcher for the BBC to working for the National Trust.

My books range from England 1050 to Texas 1848, and I can't wait for you to fall in love with my heroes and heroines!

Follow me on twitter and instagram @emilyekmurdoch, find me on facebook at facebook.com/theemilyekmurdoch, and read my blog at www.emilyekmurdoch.com.

Made in the USA
Coppell, TX
12 May 2020